"You're good with kids."

Cole had that expression on his face—she'd seen it before mostly on widowers who looked at her as though she'd be the perfect mother for their children.

Just as she expected. The equivalent of Rambo sat beside her and all he noticed were her maternal instincts. She could see the epitaph on her tombstone now: Here Lies Dependable Old Meg, Spinster. She Never Made Love, But She Was Good With Children And Animals.

Why couldn't someone—Cole, for instance—just once compliment her on something impractical? All her life she'd been dying for someone to tell her she was sexy, or provocative, or just plain pretty.

When she sighed, Cole turned and asked, "Did I say something wrong?"

Boy, did he ever.

Dear Reader,

Sometimes becoming a family takes years. But for three unlikely couples, it happens in an instant—in the new SUDDENLY...A FAMILY miniseries!

As any single parent can tell you, courtship with kids is anything but slow and easy. But three popular American Romance authors show you how much fun it can be to be caught in a "family affair."

Join Pam McCutcheon on this zany chase after a missing "baby" guaranteed to make you laugh out loud. In two months you'll be treated to Vivian Leiber's *Marrying Nicky*, and then in January don't miss Nikki Rivers's *Romancing Annie*.

Regards,

Debra Matteucci
Senior Editor & Editorial Coordinator
Harlequin Books
300 East 42nd Street
New York, NY 10017

Pam McCutcheon

CHASING BABY

Harlequin Books

TORONTO • NEW YORK • LONDON
AMSTERDAM • PARIS • SYDNEY • HAMBURG
STOCKHOLM • ATHENS • TOKYO • MILAN
MADRID • WARSAW • BUDAPEST • AUCKLAND

To Geoff and Tina Luzier for believing in me, and to the
wonderfully wyrd Paula Gill, Deb Stover, Karen Fox and
Laura Hayden for being such fabulous critique partners.
Special appreciation to Rick Watson for making me do it
right—and for making me laugh. Thanks, Doc.

ISBN 0-373-16647-8

CHASING BABY

Copyright © 1996 by Pam S. McCutcheon.

Chapter One

After a lifetime of baking cookies, being active in the 4-H and the VFW Auxiliary and baby-sitting every kid in town, Meg Hollingsworth was through being Goody Two-Shoes. She wanted to *live,* not stay buried on the rabbit farm for the rest of her life.

Exhilaration filled her as she drove into San Antonio. Finally, this was her chance to break free of Lingston, Texas. She had three days in the big city before she needed to head west to Phoenix and the Arizona State Fair. Three days, and she was going to make the absolute most of them.

She pulled her dust-covered truck into the parking lot of a hotel and checked the back. After ensuring that everything was okay there, she strode in to reserve a room.

Brimming over with excitement, she vowed not to be plain old boring Meg for the next three days. Instead, she'd be outgoing and impulsive—a free spirit, open to any adventure that came along...even if she had to make her own.

COLE MCKENZIE sighed as he skirted downtown San Antonio. What he wouldn't give for a boring, normal existence again. He had the weekend off—three whole days, and he was going to make the most of them. Finally he could relax and take a break from the constant tension and turmoil of his job on the city's vice squad.

"Daddy, look!" Luke's voice piped up from the back seat of the car as he pointed at a dog on the side of the road. "A puppy! Me have one?"

Uh-oh, not again. When his three-year-old son had his mind fixed on something, he never let go. "No, Luke, we've been over this before. I told you we just don't have the space for a dog now."

For once, Luke dropped the subject, though a glance in the rearview mirror showed the boy's lower lip extended in a full pout. Cole sighed. He wished he could give his son a puppy, but an apartment was no place for a growing dog.

Hell, it was no place for a growing boy, either. Cole's job had him working in the sleaziest neighborhoods at all hours of the night. Sometimes he didn't even know what *day* he'd be home. That was no life for a kid.

"Wanna see Mommy," Luke declared.

"Just a few more minutes, sport."

Cole spotted the hotel where his ex-wife, Natalie, had arranged to meet them, and pulled into the parking lot.

"Look, Daddy, a wed twuck."

Cole just nodded. The attractive redhead who emerged from the truck wearing tight jeans was far more interesting. He smiled in appreciation as she bounced into the hotel lobby.

"Mommy!"

Reluctantly Cole turned his gaze toward Natalie. Yep, there she was, poised attractively on the lawn, dressed in a flowing white dress and looking as though she'd just stepped off a magazine cover. She was gazing adoringly up into the eyes of her latest boyfriend, who wore a tuxedo, of all things.

Cole's mouth twitched in amusement. They looked like a matched set. Both stunningly good-looking, with sun-streaked blond hair and perfect skin, they appeared as though they belonged on top of a wedding cake.

He glanced down at his own clothing—jeans and a T-shirt, Natalie's particular bugaboos. Maybe he should feel grungy, but he didn't. He just felt comfortable—unlike the guy in the monkey suit, he was sure.

Cole parallel-parked the car at the curb behind the truck, and Luke wiggled out of his seat belt to open the car door and run across the grass to his mother. Cole followed at a more leisurely pace as he gathered the boy's small suitcase from the back seat.

The man in the monkey suit was on one knee, offering Natalie a fuzzy stuffed animal. Though the man looked silly, Cole had to give him credit—he knew just how to please the romantic in her.

Luke galloped up then, and Natalie glanced down with a smile as Luke grabbed her leg and gazed up at her. "Mommy, me have puppy?"

She gave Cole a bewildered glance, and he shook his head in negation as the other man got sheepishly to his feet.

"Now, Lukie, you know you have to ask Daddy," she said as she gave him a hug.

What was going on? Normally she kept the boy at arm's length so he wouldn't dirty her clothes. Cole's heart sank. She'd asked for additional visitation rights, too. Did she regret her decision to let Cole have custody?

"But, Mommy—"

"Here," she said, handing him the stuffed animal. "Here's a puppy. Why don't you play with this?"

Luke took the toy with poor grace and wandered across the grass to investigate the red *twuck* he'd seen earlier.

A pained look crossed the face of the other man. "But—"

"It's okay," Natalie said, patting his arm. "I know it's a bunny, but let Luke think it's a puppy for a little while."

"But I got it for you—"

Natalie smiled, but there was a thread of steel in her voice that Cole remembered well. "I know, and that was sweet of you, but we'll let Luke play with it a little bit, all right?"

It looked as though the man were going to protest again, so Cole stuck out his hand. "Hi, I'm Cole McKenzie."

Natalie clutched the other man's arm in a possessive grip. "I'm sorry, I forgot to introduce you. This is Beau Larrimer—he's the top salesman for Peterson's Jewelers.''

Beau shook Cole's hand and gave Natalie a smile as he gazed down into her eyes. "Give me time, Natty. I'm not the top yet. I only started a couple of months ago.''

She squeezed his arm. "But you're going to be, I can tell. Especially after you did so well at the bridal fair today.''

Ah, so that explained the tuxedo. Feeling a little uncomfortable around all this sweetness and light, Cole glanced around for his son. Naturally, the active boy was trying to climb into the back of the truck. "Hey, sport, get down from there and come and say goodbye.''

His son good-naturedly jumped down and ran to tackle Cole around the legs. Luke looked up and grinned an endearing smile that Natalie had always said was a perfect copy of Cole's. "Bye, Daddy.''

What a wonderful kid. He deserved better than a father with a job that could leave him an orphan at any time. That was something Cole planned to correct...soon.

He bent down to give Luke a hug and place the suitcase in his little hand. Not very good at voicing his feelings, he put all his affection into a simple kiss on the boy's forehead. Ruffling Luke's silky dark hair, Cole said, "I'll be back to pick you up Sunday night, okay?''

"Okay," Luke said, though his voice trembled.

"Don't worry, sport. It won't be very long." Cole swallowed hard. This was difficult for him, too.

Beau cleared his throat. "Uh, can I speak to you before you go?"

Cole gave Luke another hug and got to his feet. "Sure. What about?"

Beau drew him over to the side, out of earshot of Natalie and Luke. "Look, man, I'd appreciate it if you'd pick him up early, you know."

"Why?"

"Well, I kind of want to ask Natty an important question, and the kid will be in the way. You understand, don't you?"

Cole glanced at Natalie and frowned. Yeah, he understood, all right . . . and he suddenly had the uneasy feeling he knew why she'd been acting more maternal lately.

He stalled, glancing back at the parking lot as he heard a door slam.

Beau filled the stretching silence anxiously. "C'mon, man. You know how a kid can put a damper on a romantic evening."

Oh, yeah. This was just the ticket. Having Beau spend the weekend with the active three-year-old might change the man's mind about having Luke live with them if they married.

As an engine flared to life behind them, Cole smiled and slapped Beau on the back. "Sorry, man, can't help you. I've got plans this weekend myself." He backed away, still smiling.

"But—"

Just then, the redhead came running out of the hotel, screaming, "That's my truck!" She pointed at the vehicle, which was laying rubber as it sped out of the parking lot. "Stop him—he's got Baby!"

Cole swiftly put two and two together. Someone was stealing this woman's truck—*and* her baby. He grabbed his badge from his front pocket and flashed it at her. "I'm a cop. I'll get him."

Her eyes widened, and she hesitated. Then, her mouth flaring in a strange and wondrous smile, she gave him a curt nod. "Okay, let's go."

He paused, one hand on his car's door. "No. You stay here."

She yanked open the passenger door and hopped in. "There's no way you're going without me."

Cole frowned and slid behind the steering wheel. "You can't come."

"Why not?"

"It's dangerous."

"So?"

Her expression was determined, set. He could tell she wasn't going to budge an inch. Damn. Taking a civilian on a high-speed chase was dumb, but he had no time to argue—and it *was* her baby.

Shaking his head, Cole said, "Okay, but you do exactly as I say. Agreed?"

"Okay, okay. Just hurry!"

Slamming the car into gear, Cole obliged, peeling out of the parking lot. As they pursued the stolen truck, Cole allowed himself one glance back and grinned. Beau was standing openmouthed, staring after them, one hand raised as if in protest.

BEAU FROWNED after Natty's ex-husband. Damn. Now he and Natty were stuck with the kid all weekend. Just what he didn't need.

He glanced over at her. She was so lovely, he'd been overcome, unable to resist playing to her fantasies by trying to be the ultimate romantic. And look where it had gotten him—acting like a fool in front of her ex-husband as he knelt to propose to her. Speaking of which, where was that bunny?

He glanced around swiftly, then straightened as his boss came hurrying out of the hotel.

"Thank heaven I caught you," Mr. Peterson said, panting from the exertion.

"Yes, sir? I thought the bridal fair was over for the day."

"It is, it is." He glanced at Natalie and pulled Beau aside to whisper to him. "But when you packed up the wedding sets, you took the wrong engagement ring for your girlfriend."

"The wrong one?" He couldn't have.

"Yes, I found the seven-carat cubic zirconia while I was checking the inventory, so you must have taken the seven-carat diamond by mistake."

Beau swallowed hard. Ah, hell, he must have gotten them mixed up at the bridal fair. He wasn't experienced enough to know the difference between a diamond and a CZ yet, but he'd wanted to impress Natty with something big and spectacular. And since he couldn't afford a real diamond, he'd gotten the emerald-cut CZ.

He figured he'd explain it to her once she was properly impressed—and replace it with the real thing once he made his mark with the company. By then, she'd be so in love with him, he knew she'd understand. He doubted she'd be so understanding now.

Okay, he'd figure something out—but first he had to get the ring back. "It's all right, sir, I'll switch it back."

Mr. Peterson released a sigh of relief. "Good. Can I have it now?"

"Sure." Beau glanced around for the little boy. "Hey, kid."

"His name is Luke," Natty reminded him with a thread of exasperation in her voice.

"Right. Luke." The boy glanced up at him with a wary look in his eyes, and Beau noticed with rising panic that Luke no longer had the stuffed animal in his arms. Beau cursed inwardly. Damn his stupid romantic impulse—why had he tied the ring to a ribbon around the bunny's neck? And why in hell had Natty given it to her son?

Seeing his career going down in flames, Beau knelt to stare the boy straight in the eyes, and asked in his most commanding tone, "Where's the bunny?"

The kid's face screwed up like he was going to start bawling. Natty didn't look very happy with Beau, either, so he tried to restrain the anger in his voice. "I'm sorry, Luke, but I have to know where the bunny is."

The kid sniffled. "Don't have it!" he wailed.

"Where'd you put it?" Beau asked through clenched teeth, his patience almost gone.

"Dint *have* bunny." Luke turned to bury his face in his mother's dress.

Natalie knelt down next to her son, giving Beau an annoyed glare. "He doesn't know it's a bunny."

Beau fumed. Damn it, this was important.

"It's okay, Lukie," she said. "Uncle Beau was talking about the puppy. You know the toy puppy I gave you?"

Luke stuck three fingers in his mouth and sniveled as he gave Beau a sidelong glance and nodded.

"Where is the puppy now, Lukie?"

"Don't know."

Luke began to cry in earnest, and Beau slapped his thigh in exasperation. "Damn it, Natty, I need that bunny."

She and Mr. Peterson looked at him as though he were crazy. Beau gestured helplessly. "The ring was around its neck, sir."

Mr. Peterson didn't look any more enlightened—or mollified. "Well, get it *back*. Now."

"Ring?" Natty asked.

Hell, he didn't want to propose to her in front of his boss and the kid. "Yes, a ring. It was a...a present for you. I tied it to the ribbon around the bunny's neck, and now it's gone." He glared down at the kid. "And Luke can't remember where it is."

Beau turned to stare down at Luke, who looked scared. As well he should. If he'd lost that ring...

Natty picked Luke up, giving Beau a glare. "You've probably terrified him so much he won't remember." Turning to Luke, she said, "It's okay, sweetie. Do you remember where you put the puppy?"

Luke shook his head, his fingers still in his mouth and his eyes downcast as Beau fumed in helpless rage and Mr. Peterson paced, flashing them irate glances.

Natty prodded Luke some more. "Did you drop it in the flowers?"

He shook his head again. As Natty continued playing twenty questions with the boy without success, Beau tried to remember how much a seven-carat diamond cost. The blood drained from his head. Far more than he could afford. Damn it, his life would be ruined if they didn't find that bunny. He gave Natty an agonized, pleading look.

Natty shrugged helplessly and turned to her son again. "This is important, Luke. We're going to spend the weekend with Uncle Beau, and we have to find that puppy for him, okay?"

Luke nodded, but still wouldn't meet anyone's eyes.

"Think, honey. Where did you put the puppy? Did you put it in someone's car?"

Luke nodded again. Finally, they were getting somewhere. "Which car?" Beau demanded.

The kid turned to look at him. Though he was pouting, Beau could have sworn there was a gleam in his eyes as he announced, "Daddy's."

"Daddy's car?" Natty gave Beau a triumphant look. "You put it in Daddy's car?"

Luke nodded, and Beau's hopes rose. "Well, come on, then. If we hurry, we might be able to catch them." He rushed Natty and her kid toward the car and fussed until they were strapped in.

Lunging in behind the wheel, he yelled, "Don't worry, Mr. Peterson, I'll get that ring back for you."

His boss's countenance was set and hard. "You'd better, Larrimer. If we don't get that ring back by tomorrow, it's your job."

"Yes, *sir,*" he called out the window as he sped out of the parking lot.

"You're crazy," Natty said. "You'll never catch Cole. You don't even know where he went."

"Oh, yes, I do. When he left, he was heading west on I-10. If he hasn't gotten off, I'll catch up to him. I have to."

"You have to? Why?"

"Because he has the bunny with the ring."

"So can't you wait until he picks Luke up on Sunday and get the bunny then?"

"No, I can't. You heard Mr. Peterson. If I don't get that ring back to the store by tomorrow, I'll lose my job."

Natty looked puzzled. "But I thought you said it was a present for me."

Beau frowned. How was he going to explain this without mentioning the proposal, or the fact that he'd been about to give her a fake diamond instead of the real thing? Great. Now everything was ruined.

MEG SCANNED the dense weekend traffic anxiously. All her dreams were driving away in that truck. She couldn't afford to lose it, not after all she'd gone through to get Pops to finally agree to the bet.

Suddenly she spotted the truck and pointed. "There it is—in the left lane."

"I see it," the man said.

For the first time since she'd jumped into the car, Meg relaxed a bit. She could see her truck in the distance, and it was only a matter of time until they overtook it, thanks to the fast driving of her rescuer.

Now that she had a moment, she glanced at him. Lord, she'd been so anxious to go on an adventure that she hadn't questioned anything, but had just jumped into the car with a total stranger.

And a very good-looking stranger at that. With his short black hair, smoldering dark eyes in a chiseled, tanned face and lean, hard physique, he looked like danger personified.

Her heart skipped a beat. Here at last was the embodiment of all those dark and dangerous heroes she loved in romance novels. She gulped. Was she ready for this? Her heart raced. She wasn't sure whether it was from excitement or from fear, but she didn't care. She'd gone looking for adventure, and it appeared she'd found it.

But, just in case...it wouldn't hurt to know a little more about him. "Uh, thanks for doing this. By the way, I'm Meg Hollingsworth."

"Cole McKenzie," he grunted as he changed lanes and sped up. "You know, you shouldn't leave your keys in the ignition."

That was no way for a hero to talk.

She stared at him indignantly, her illusions shattered. "I didn't. He must have hot-wired it or something. I still have my keys." She fished around in her purse until she found her key ring.

She dangled them in front of his face. "See? You know, you shouldn't make assumptions like that."

"Sorry."

Somewhat mollified, Meg settled back in her seat and tossed her keys into her purse, missing the first part of his question.

"... baby alone in the truck?" His voice sounded hard, accusing.

"Well, it was only for a few minutes, while I registered at the hotel. I wasn't gone that long, and I certainly didn't expect anyone to steal him."

"You'd be surprised at what people would steal in this town." He gave her a sidelong, censuring glance. "Even children."

Children, yes. And trucks, too—obviously. But...
"I don't see why anyone else would want him," she said frankly.

He gave her a disgusted look. "You're some mother—"

Shocked, Meg said, "Watch it, bud. There's no reason to call me names, even if you are a cop." A thought suddenly occurred to her. "You *are* a cop, aren't you?"

He grimaced as he switched lanes and sped forward to the next bottleneck on the highway. "Hell of a time to ask that now. Yeah, I'm a cop. You saw my badge, remember?"

"Yes, but I didn't get a very good look at it. Could I see it again, please?"

He sighed and dug the badge out of his tight jeans, then tossed it to her. She opened the well-worn case and inspected the badge. It certainly looked authentic.

"Satisfied?" he asked.

She handed it back. "Yes, thank you." After all, what were the odds of him carrying a fake police badge in his pocket, just waiting for screaming women to come running up to him so he could steal them away in his car? Not very high. No, the badge was probably authentic.

He shoved it back in his pocket and kept his gaze focused on the traffic. Good—that was what she wanted him to do, concentrate on closing as much distance between them and the truck as possible.

They were only a few car lengths away now and, impatient to get this over with, Meg asked, "Why isn't he driving any faster?"

"He probably didn't expect anyone to follow him. Most people whose cars are stolen don't—they can't."

"Oh. Of course."

"And since he's been in the left lane of the freeway the whole time, I'd say he's planning on hightailing it out of town before anyone reports the truck stolen. He's not driving fast because he can't afford to get stopped for speeding."

Good—then they had an excellent chance of catching him and regaining her truck and Baby.

Cole glanced in the rearview mirror. "Ah, hell."

"What is it?"

"A cop—unfortunately, he just caught *us* speeding."

Meg turned around to see and sure enough, a patrol car was on their tail, lights flashing.

Cole slowed down and pulled into the right lane.

"Wait," she said, reaching toward the wheel. "What are you doing?"

"We're being pulled over."

"So what? You're a cop, aren't you?"

He frowned at her. "Yes, but that doesn't make me above the law. If I don't stop now, they might think I'm guilty of something besides speeding. Don't worry, I'll explain everything and we'll be on our way in no time."

Not at all reassured, Meg frowned and fidgeted as they pulled off the road and the patrol car pulled up behind them. Cole got out of the car, his badge extended.

Meg suddenly realized they'd catch the crook much faster if they were in a real police car. Excited, she got out of the car to add her persuasion to Cole's.

Apparently having established his bona fides, Cole was saying, "...in pursuit of the kidnapper who stole her vehicle and her son from a hotel parking lot."

Startled, Meg said, "My son? Where'd you get that idea?"

Cole turned to frown at her. "From you. You said he stole your baby."

Uh-oh—that explained a few of his earlier remarks. She gave him what had to be a sick-looking smile. "Uh, sorry for the confusion. It's not my baby. He stole *Baby,* my prize rabbit. He was in a cage in the back of the truck...."

Her voice trailed off as the patrolman barked with laughter. "You mean to say you're chasing a bunny-napper?"

Cole glared at him. "It's not funny, Garcia. I thought—"

Garcia chuckled. "Oh yeah, I can see where a fuzzy little rabbit would look just like a little boy—especially since it was in a cage and all. Wait until the guys in Vice hear about this." He dissolved into laughter.

Cole just glowered at her, no doubt for making him look like a fool in front of one of his peers.

"Yeah, I know," Meg said. "Real funny. But the fact is, Baby has been stolen and I want him back."

Garcia wiped his eyes. "I'm sorry, ma'am. I don't know of any laws against stealing bunnies."

His own wit—or half-wit, if the look on Cole's face was any judge—started the man laughing again.

"What about stealing trucks?"

The man sobered. "True, there is a law against that. But he's out of the city limits by now—and out of our jurisdiction. If you'd like to file a report . . ."

"I don't have time for that." She turned to Cole. "C'mon, let's go get him."

He gave her a disgusted look. "You want me to chase after a rabbit?"

"Yes, please. It's a very valuable rabbit."

Garcia chortled again, and Cole just glared at her.

"C'mon," she pleaded. "He stole my truck, too, remember? Help me get it back, please."

Cole frowned. "I'm not..." He glanced past her at a white sports car that had driven up behind the patrol car. "Ah, hell."

"What is it?" Meg asked.

Cole grimaced as a man and a woman got out of the car and approached them. "It's my ex-wife and her boyfriend."

Garcia snickered. "Oh, this is getting good."

Puzzled, Meg turned to Cole. "What are they doing here?"

"Hell if I know, but whatever it is, it isn't good."

"Beau, don't be a fool," the woman was saying.

"Nonsense," the man in the tuxedo declared. "Officer—" he pointed dramatically at Cole "—arrest that man."

Startled, Garcia asked, "Why?"

"He stole my bunny!"

It was too much for the poor patrolman, who burst into fresh gales of laughter.

Chapter Two

Cole rolled his eyes heavenward. How did he get himself in these situations? And how could he get himself out? His instincts told him there was something strange about this whole thing.

He let out a short bark of laughter. Oh, yeah, that took great instincts—just look around him. As Beau tried to get the chuckling Garcia's attention, Natalie tugged at Beau's arm, trying to get him to shut up. Meg just stood there, looking up at Cole as if he were the answer to her prayers.

"Can we *go* now?" she asked.

His gaze roamed back to her heart-shaped face. Her bright blue eyes, milky complexion and tangle of red curls atop a slender body were hard to resist—and so was the pleading expression she'd turned on him.

Cole steeled himself against her attraction. That was no reason to get involved, especially since there was obviously something strange going on here. Until he found out what it was, he'd be better off if he just kept his guard up.

He jerked his head toward Beau. "He seems to think it's his rabbit we're chasing. How do you explain that?"

She shrugged, seeming to do the simple action with her entire body, and making the slight curves under her simple cotton shirt move in interesting ways. "I don't know. I've never seen that man before in my life. If you ask me, he's crazy."

Cole glanced at Beau, who was arguing with the chuckling cop. She had a point. Cole frowned, trying to make sense of it all.

"Look," Meg said. "As soon as we catch up to my truck, I can show you Baby's papers and prove he's mine, okay?"

That was right, he'd seen her getting out of the truck. Chances were, the truck belonged to her. If it did, then the rabbit probably did, too.

Damn, what was he getting himself into? All he'd wanted to do was escape Beau's presence, do a good deed for a pretty stranger, then get on with deciding whether or not to take the position he'd been offered. How had it gotten all bollixed up like this?

"Cole?" Meg asked, almost squirming in her haste to be gone. "He's getting farther away with every second."

She was right. And, hell, his objectives hadn't changed—he still wanted to help Meg and get away from Beau.

He turned to where Beau and Garcia were arguing, while Natalie looked on in ill-concealed impatience.

"...don't care about the bunny," Beau said. "I just want what's attached to it."

Meg glanced at him in disgust. "Listen, buddy, if you want fur that bad, I'll sell you some—but you can't have my rabbit."

Beau looked as though he were reaching the end of his rope. "It's . . . not . . . your . . . rabbit. It's *mine.*"

Garcia had lost his earlier merriment, and now seemed totally confused—not to mention exasperated. Hoping to rescue his fellow police officer and get out of there with his own sanity intact, Cole said, "I can clear this up."

Garcia looked doubtful. "I certainly hope so."

"The rabbit is in the truck we're following," Cole explained. "And as soon as we catch up to it, I'll ascertain the rightful owner and make sure that person gets it back. All right?"

Meg shouted, "Yes!" at the same time Beau shouted, "No!"

Meg rolled her eyes in exasperation. "C'mon, Cole. Let's go."

"No!" Beau insisted. "It's in your car."

Beau was obviously losing it if he thought Cole had a rabbit in his car. Meg looked at Beau as if he were deranged, and Cole signaled Garcia with his eyes. Garcia nodded in comprehension, and Cole headed toward the car. "All right, let's go."

"No!" Beau yelled. "Don't let them get away with my bunny!" He lunged toward Cole, but Garcia restrained him, saying, "It's all right, let's just make a full report. . . ."

EXCITEMENT filled Meg as she and Cole raced toward his car and hopped in. "It's about time," she said. "Let's get him."

Cole obligingly stepped on the gas, and they were finally on their way after Baby again.

She glanced down at the console. He was living up to her expectations now, she thought approvingly as the needle on the speedometer crept toward seventy-five. A little thrill arced through her. She'd always wanted to meet a man like the poet Byron—"mad, bad, and dangerous to know." Was that Cole? She hoped so.

For a few moments there, when he seemed intent on stopping the chase, she'd doubted it, but this was more like it. Maybe the weekend wouldn't be a waste after all. She watched the needle creep higher. So long as they weren't arrested, that is. "Careful—we might get stopped for speeding again."

"It's okay. Garcia will get on the horn and let everyone know to be on the lookout for your truck—and explain who I am. He'll also delay Beau long enough for us to get away clean."

She nodded, and Cole glanced at her, suspicion written on his face. "Are you sure you've never met him before?"

"I'm positive," Meg said. "He has the kind of smooth good looks you don't forget easily." Smooth and bland, just like a slice of pristine white bread that made you want to slap a dollop of mustard on it, just to make it look a little less perfect.

Cole snorted. "Smooth. Yeah. So why does he claim the rabbit is his?"

"Heck if I know—he's your friend, not mine."

"He's not my friend." Cole gritted the words through his teeth. "He's my ex-wife's boyfriend. Probably her soon-to-be-husband."

Ah, so he was jealous. Meg knew just how he felt— she'd read about it often enough. Patting his arm, she said, "I understand. You're upset because you want her back, but she just can't handle the dangerous life you lead, so she spurned you."

"What? Where do you get your ideas? Soap operas?"

Meg felt her cheeks warm, and knew she was blushing. It was the curse of fair skin. "No," she said vehemently. "I don't watch soap operas."

He snorted in disbelief.

"Well, maybe a couple, but only about once a week." It wasn't like she was addicted or anything. "No, I read. Perhaps you've heard of it? Words written in ink on paper? Books?" She grabbed one out of her voluminous purse and waved it at him.

He glanced at the romance novel she was waving in his face. "Oh, yeah. Romance. Like *there's* a real connection to reality."

She turned to face him then, twisting to the limits of the seat belt. She'd been faced with detractors before, and she knew just how to handle them. "And how many have *you* read?"

"None. I don't need to—I know what's in them."

She gave him plenty of rope to hang himself. "Oh, and what's that?"

"A man and a woman meet, fall in love, get married and live happily ever after. Right?"

Her indignation cooled somewhat. That wasn't exactly what she'd expected to hear. "Well, yes, in the most simplistic terms, that's true of most romance novels. What's wrong with that?"

"It's not real."

"Not real? What do you mean?"

"Look, real life isn't like that. You meet someone, fall in love, get married, and then the problems start. You find out he isn't the white knight you thought, and she's no sweet princess. You argue, you fight, you break up. That's real life. Haven't you figured that out yet?"

Her gaze fixed on the book she still held in her hand, Meg murmured, "No, I haven't. I've never been in love." Oh, she'd wanted to be, but she'd never met a man who made her feel the sort of all-consuming passion she'd read about.

She could feel Cole's start of surprise as he turned to stare at her. "Never?"

She shook her head. Only in her dreams.

"Are the men in your town blind?"

Meg shrugged off the question. She'd learned the hard way that the only men who were ever interested in her were widowers looking for a mother for their children. She loved kids, but she planned to take Gram's advice and ensure she didn't settle for anything less than love. Without it, she knew she'd be unhappy, forever barefoot and pregnant and midwifing endless litters of rabbits.

No, Cole was just being kind. She gave him a speculative glance. Maybe he wasn't the tortured man she'd thought, but that didn't mean he wasn't still hero material.

Cole scanned the road ahead of him. "Well, don't worry about it. Love isn't all it's cracked up to be."

He had to be wrong—romances wouldn't sell so well if there wasn't some basic truth there somewhere. "Well, you're welcome to your opinion, but I'll take my chances, thank you."

He shrugged. "It's your life."

That's right, and she was doing all she could to get control of it. "Damn straight. But if we don't catch Baby, my chances of ever finding anything resembling a life are remote."

"Why is this rabbit so important?"

"Because I have a bet with my grandfather." Disappointed that Cole didn't seem to be living up to the role of hero in her little fantasy, she asked, "What do you care? In case you've forgotten, we're in a chase here, not a cocktail party." She peered out the window. "Where is that truck, anyway?"

Cole grimaced. "Look, I'm doing the best I can in this weekend traffic. If your thief is still on I-10, we'll catch him, don't worry. Until then, I'd like to know a little more about why I'm doing this, to see if this wildgoose—or rather rabbit—chase is worth the trouble. Okay?"

She sighed. True, she owed him an explanation. It was the least she could do. "Okay."

"So what's this about a bet?"

"Well, in order to understand it, you have to know what my life has been like up to now."

"Go on." He didn't sound leery, but that was only because he didn't know just how boring her life was.

"Well, my parents died in a car accident when I was six, so my older brother and I went to live with Pops and Gram on their rabbit farm." She grimaced in distaste.

"I take it you don't care for the rabbit farm?"

"Oh, I thought it was terrific. All those soft, furry bunnies seemed like wonderful playmates, until I learned Pops raised them for their meat and hides."

"I see," he said in a flat tone, but Meg could tell he thought she was a bit soft in the heart—and the head.

"I was a little upset when I heard he killed them for money, but what could I do?"

"What did you do?" Cole asked, appearing genuinely curious.

"Well, when I got a little older, Gram encouraged me to get involved in the community. In the small town I grew up in, everyone knows everyone else, and I jumped right in—organized charity drives, baked cookies, baby-sat, everything. I got real involved." Too involved. Now it seemed the townspeople couldn't live without her. It was hell being indispensable.

Her sadness must have echoed in her voice, for Cole said, "What's wrong with that?"

"Nothing, but everyone sees me as the town drudge or something. 'Just ask dependable old Meg—she'll do it.'"

"And you don't like being 'dependable old Meg'?"

She gave him an indignant glance. "What woman would? Being dependable is a curse. I worked my butt off, but never got invited to a football game because everyone knew I'd be selling refreshments for the booster club. I was always busy baby-sitting some-one's kids on the weekends, so I hardly ever got asked out. And no one invited me to the high school prom, because they knew I'd be too busy working behind the scenes to spend much time with a date."

"Then they were fools."

Startled out of her self-pity, Meg said, "I beg your pardon?"

"The boys in your town must have been fools to have ignored you."

She felt herself blush again, not knowing how to take his compliment. "I...I... Thank you."

"You're welcome. So what does this have to do with the bet?"

"Well, as you can imagine, I've been wanting out of that town forever. I've never had any excitement or real fun in my life, so I've been saving money for years. As soon as I turned eighteen, I planned to hightail it out of there and move to San Antonio, where I wouldn't be 'dependable old Meg' anymore."

"Why didn't you?"

She sighed, even as her gaze continually scanned the traffic ahead for her truck. "When I was seventeen, Gram died." And with her had gone most of the joy in Meg's life. "That was nine years ago. Pops just kind of fell apart after that, and he needed me around to take care of him. You know, run the house, cook his meals, make sure he takes his medicine, that sort of thing. I can't leave."

"What about your brother? Can't he help?"

"Jerry? Oh, he takes care of the rabbit farm all right, but he has no concept of what Pops needs. And he gets so caught up in racing his silly cars that he sometimes forgets about Pops. I'm afraid to leave them alone for long, for fear of what will happen to my grandfather."

And the rabbit farm was getting to be too much for Pops to handle, which was another reason she wanted to move to San Antonio. That way she could keep an eye on Pops and he'd have access to the best medical facilities.

"Are you sure about that? Sounds like they're taking advantage of you."

She nodded. "Unfortunately, I am sure. I left for a week to visit some relatives in Arizona, and Jerry forgot to give Pops his medication. He ended up in the hospital."

"I'm sorry," Cole said, his voice full of compassion.

Compassion in a bad boy? Not in the novels she'd read. It looked like Cole wasn't exactly the hero she'd envisioned. She shrugged. "It's okay, I'm used to it. But I haven't given up yet. A couple of years ago, I started raising Angora rabbits instead, hoping Pops would switch to them." If she couldn't get him to move, at least she could get him to slow down—raising Angoras would be a lot easier on him.

"I thought a rabbit was a rabbit."

"Oh, no, not at all. There are many different kinds. Angora rabbits have long, silky fur that you harvest by shearing or pulling. It doesn't harm the rabbit, and there's quite a market for the fur in knit goods—sweaters, hats, muffs, that sort of thing.''

"And Pops doesn't like the Angoras?"

She slumped in the seat. "You got that right. He thinks they're silly creatures, good for nothing but looking pretty. So I've been trying to prove him wrong.''

"How?"

She glanced at him, and grinned as she remembered how she'd tricked her grandfather. "Well, he scoffed once too often, so I bet him one of my rabbits could win the title of grand champion within a year. If I win, Pops will sell the rabbit farm and move to San Antonio. If I lose, I promised never to mention San Antonio again.''

"And you won?"

"Not yet—the year's almost up, but my prize rabbit only has to win one more competition to be named grand champion.''

"That's Baby?"

"Right. I was on the way to the Arizona State Fair in Phoenix when he was stolen. If I lose him, I lose the bet.'' And with it, all her chances of escaping Lingston.

Meg leaned forward and pointed. "Hey, what's that?"

"What?"

"There in the distance. What's that red spot? Looks like it could be my truck.''

"Could be," Cole conceded, and sped up as they flashed by a sign that proclaimed that the next exit was Kerrville. "What town do you live in, anyway?"

"Oh, you've probably never heard of it. Lingston."

"Lingston?" Cole turned to look at her in surprise. Simultaneously, a sudden noise came from the back seat that sounded like a sneeze.

Obviously startled, Cole jerked the wheel to the right. The wheels caught on the gravel alongside the road, and the car swerved, hitting a speed-limit sign.

Meg's heart leaped into her throat as the car came to a sudden jolting stop. She couldn't help letting out a shriek. "What was that?"

A small wail sounded from the back seat, and Meg twisted to see a small dark-haired boy staring up at her from the floorboards, his eyes widened with alarm.

"Luke!" Cole jerked the back door open. "Are you all right?"

"Daddy!" cried the little boy, and held his hands out to Cole.

Meg stared in dismay and wonder. This was the last straw. Dark, dangerous heroes did *not* come accompanied by small children.

"He looks fine to me," she said. "He's probably just scared." And it appeared he'd been protected down on the floorboards.

Cole glared at her. "What do you know?"

"Quite a lot, actually. I teach the Red Cross child-care course." She softened her tone, knowing Cole was just concerned about his son.

"Oh, yeah. Dependable Meg."

She winced. The way he said it, it sounded like an epithet. Well, that was how she thought of it, too, so why did it hurt so much when he said it?

Luke released his choke hold on Cole and said, "Me okay, Daddy."

"Good. Now how in the...tarnation did you get in the back seat?"

Luke pouted and looked up with a guilty expression. "P'liceman."

"You got out of the car when we all stopped to talk to the policeman?"

Luke nodded.

"Does Mommy know you're here?"

Eyes downcast, Luke shook his head.

Cole sighed. "Wonderful," he muttered. Turning back to Luke, he said, "You know Mommy is going to be very worried about you. You shouldn't have done that, Luke."

The boy's lower lip started quivering, and Cole sighed again. "Why, sport? Why'd you do it?"

"Unca Beau *mean,*" Luke declared, with all the force in his small body.

"'Uncle' Beau?" Cole swore softly, but visibly struggled to control his temper around his son. "Yeah, well, I can't blame you there."

"Is it wise to bad-mouth his mother's boyfriend?" Meg asked.

Cole glared at her as he strapped Luke in the back seat and admonished him to be still. "Doesn't look as though Beau needs any help from me to get on Luke's bad side," Cole said in a clipped tone. "Besides, I'm beginning to wonder if there isn't something... strange about Beau. I'm not sure I want my son anywhere near him. Natalie isn't exactly the best judge of character."

So what did that say about Cole? Natalie had chosen him as a husband at one time.

As Cole checked the damage to his car, Meg contemplated what nefarious deeds Beau might be responsible for. "What do you think he did?" she asked.

Cole slammed Luke's door and got back in the car, strapping himself in. Lowering his voice, he said, "I don't know, but when he said he wanted something that was attached to the rabbit, I don't think he meant the fur."

"You think he tied something to Baby? What?" Would it harm Baby—or his fur? She hoped not—his long, silky fur promised to be her salvation, if it would win him grand champion status. "And why?"

Cole shrugged. "I don't know. Since Beau knew I was dropping Luke off, maybe he decided to hide something until after I left."

Horrified, yet excited at the same time, Meg drew in a sharp breath. "You mean... like drugs or something?"

"Maybe. In my line of work, I've seen it happen often enough. You notice he didn't say *what* he tied to the rabbit."

Meg nodded. "Because you and Garcia were there."

"Maybe. In any case, Luke is well out of it."

Meg cast a glance back at the little boy, who seemed to be having a hard time keeping his eyes open. A father's love was something she could understand.

He put the keys in the ignition, and she was pleasantly surprised when the engine flared to life. "Let's see if this thing will move."

The car moved in reverse, then Cole put it into drive. It shuddered forward in fits and starts and clanked back onto the highway. Cole swore under his breath.

"What's wrong with it?"

"The fender's bent, and the front end's way out of alignment. I can't drive it this way—I have to get to a service station."

No! Meg cried in silent frustration. And just when they'd been so close to catching the thief again.

Cole gave her an apologetic glance. "I'm sorry. But don't worry, I'll help you file a report—"

"No, that's okay." There was no way she'd let a little thing like this stop her. Her mind started working furiously, trying to figure out how she could continue this chase. She'd come too close to lose her dream without a fight. "I'll figure out something else."

"Like what?" Cole's tone was skeptical.

"I don't know...." First, she needed a car. Rent one? No, that would take too long, and she didn't want to use Pops's credit card. She was going to win this bet without relying on him in any way. How else, then? Borrow one? She knew people all over Texas....

Suddenly she snapped her fingers. "Glenda."

"Glenda?" Cole asked as he steered the limping car off the freeway and into Kerrville.

"Glenda is my cousin. She lives here and has two cars. I bet she'd loan me one."

"What? You're crazy, you know that?"

"No, not crazy. Determined."

"I stand by my word choice," he said with a wry look. "What would *you* call a person who wants to go chasing after a potentially dangerous felon? One who very likely has illegal narcotics stashed on him?''

He had a point—she hadn't stopped to think about what kind of person might have taken off with her truck. "You think the thief knew what was in with Baby?"

He shrugged and pulled into a service station. "It's possible."

"Well, what if it *is* drugs, and Baby eats it or something? I've got to save my rabbit."

Cole snorted in exasperation. "You're certifiable, you know that? You could get hurt."

Meg smiled. "Not if you're with me."

"Not on your life." He jerked his head toward the back seat. "I have a son to protect, remember?"

Meg chewed her lip as she glanced at Luke. The sleeping child had been so quiet, she'd forgotten. "Okay, then I'll do it without you."

Cole shook his head. "Well, I can't stop you. It's your neck."

The service station attendant gave one glance at their crumpled fender and waved them into one of the stalls. Cole retrieved the boy from the back seat. "Just don't do anything stupid, okay?"

Fuming, Meg got out of the car and searched inside her bag until she found her address book. Glancing around, she spotted a pay phone and stalked toward it. No thief or surly cop was going to stop *her* from winning that bet.

She dialed Glenda's number and sighed in relief when her cousin answered the phone. "Glenda? Hi, it's Meg. I need your help."

She explained her need to borrow Glenda's car, saying only that it was an emergency. She didn't mention thieves or bets, and she promised any favor in return. Glenda was a little reluctant, but went to talk to her husband as Meg waited.

"Meg?" came Glenda's tentative voice.

"Yes? *Can* I borrow one of your cars?"

"Were you serious about that favor?"

"Of course—anything you want. Just name it."

"Well, Dan and I have been trying for weeks to spend a romantic weekend in San Antonio, but we haven't been able to find a baby-sitter for Susie. Will you take her for a weekend?"

Meg sighed in relief. The four-year-old wasn't a problem—Meg had taken care of her often enough. "Any time. Can you bring me the car right away?"

"Sure. Where are you?"

She gave Glenda directions and hung up, feeling triumphant. Her solution was shaping up quite nicely. In fact, she was having an adventure. She laughed to herself. Yes, an adventure, and she hadn't done half-bad so far. She was beginning to think there wasn't much she couldn't handle. Maybe she wouldn't need Cole's help after all.

She wandered over to the back part of the lot, where Cole and Luke were sitting on the grass. Luke was chasing a butterfly as Cole watched.

He squinted up at her. "So?"

Feeling smug, Meg said, "The car will be here shortly. Thanks for your help."

He shrugged. "No problem. Say, could you watch Luke while I make a phone call? I have to let Natalie know where he is, before she accuses me of kidnapping or something. I'll just leave a message on her machine.''

''Sure,'' Meg said. It was the least she could do. After all, Cole had tried to catch the thief for her. He couldn't help it if his son had crawled into the car—and she couldn't blame him for not wanting to put the little boy in danger.

''Luke, stay here and mind Meg, okay?''

Luke gave her a devilish grin. '''Kay.''

Oh, my, this little boy was going to be quite a little charmer when he grew up—just like his daddy. Luke swooped for another butterfly, and Meg turned her gaze toward the elder McKenzie. She suspected Cole could be a charmer if he wanted to—he just didn't seem to want to bother with her.

She sighed. It was the story of her life. Just once, she'd like to be swept off her feet by a dashing rogue and experience all those frightening, exhilarating sensations her books described. She'd cast Cole in the part of the hero, but he wasn't following his cues. He was supposed to strip her naked with his gaze, showing unbridled passion as he fought unsuccessfully to keep his hands from her warm, willing body.

Instead, his incredulous gaze stripped all illusions from her mind, and he seemed perfectly able to keep his hands off her. Damn. And he was so good-looking, too. Oh, well, it was hard to cast him as dark and dangerous when he showed such tenderness toward his son.

The mechanic came out, wiping his hands on a greasy rag, and approached Cole. They spoke for a few moments, and then Cole came back to join them as the station attendant backed the car out to a parking spot outside the station.

"How's the car?" she asked.

Cole levered himself down on the grass. "Not good. Just as I thought, the front end is way out of alignment and the tie-rod's bent. He's busy right now, so it'll take a day or two to fix it."

"I'm sorry. Is there anything I can do?"

He quirked a smile at her. "You could give me a ride back to San Antonio."

She shook her head. "You know I can't do that. I have to find Baby. Every moment I waste here is one more moment he gets farther away."

He nodded. "I know. Don't worry about it. Say, are you really from Lingston?"

"Yes—" Suddenly she spotted Glenda's car. Standing, she waved her over. Glenda pulled up next to them, with Susie in the back seat. Her husband was in the car behind them, ready to give Glenda a ride home.

Glenda got out of the car, smiling, and tossed Meg her keys. "There you go. All ready."

"Thanks," Meg said with heartfelt relief. "I owe you one."

Glenda grinned. "Not anymore, you don't." She headed toward her husband's car. "We'll be home Sunday after two. Give me a call and let me know when you're coming by."

Meg glanced in the back seat. "Wait. Don't you think you're forgetting something?"

"No, what?"

Meg chuckled. "Your daughter, silly. Remember Susie?"

Glenda just laughed as she continued toward the other car. "She's yours for the weekend...just as you promised."

"But I—"

Glenda hopped in. "Don't worry—her things are in the trunk. See you Sunday."

Before Meg could say another word, Glenda and Dan roared off in their car. As she stood there, open-mouthed, Cole approached. "What was that all about?"

"I promised my cousin I'd keep Susie for a week-end, but I didn't know she meant *this* weekend."

"So they conned you, huh?" Cole grinned then. It was the first honest-to-God smile she'd seen on his face, and Meg's stomach flipped in reaction. Stop that, she admonished her unruly body. It didn't know yet what her mind understood all too well—that this man wasn't interested in her.

Meg smiled ruefully. "Yeah, they conned me. Now what am I going to do about Baby?"

"Nothing you *can* do."

"Maybe. Maybe not." She glanced over at Susie, who was waving her arms and trying hard to figure out how to get out the safety-locked door. "Say, could you watch both kids while I—?"

"No way. This is the first time off I've had in weeks, and I need the time to find out more about Lingston. One kid is bad enough, but two? I don't think so."

"Lingston? Why would anyone want to know about Lingston?"

He shrugged. "Does it matter?"

"No, I guess not." She stuck out her hand. "Well, thanks for all your help. Wish me luck."

He took her hand and regarded her seriously. So seriously that Meg's heart beat a little faster. Hell, even if he wasn't the tortured hero she was looking for, she could pretend, couldn't she? She might even give up the chase for Baby if she could exchange it for one mad fling. Was he—?

Staring straight into her eyes, he said, "This is a dumb thing to do."

Her hopes plummeted, and she jerked her hand back. What did she expect, anyway?

"If I wanted your opin—"

Quickly Cole grabbed her shoulder and pulled her down to crouch next to the car, snagging Luke, as well.

"Quiet," he said.

"What are you doing?" she said through clenched teeth. "Let go of me."

"All right," he whispered. "But keep your voice—and your head—down. They're here."

What? "Who's here?"

"Beau and Natalie." Luke started to dart off after another butterfly, but Cole caught him and slung the child up onto his back, saying, "Let's play piggyback."

Still crouched down behind Glenda's car, Meg asked, "So? Why are we hiding?"

Cole grimaced. "I'd just as soon not have to live through another scene, thank you. Besides, maybe if Beau doesn't know I'm watching him, he'll slip up."

He rose slowly to peer through the car windows, Luke gleefully kicking him in the ribs.

"What are they doing?" Meg whispered.

"Getting gas," Cole said. "Ah, hell, they spotted my car."

Meg risked a peek through the car windows herself. Beau grabbed the station attendant and pointed at Cole's car, gesturing wildly. The man shrugged him off, and Beau slammed back in the car, then drove off to the side and parked.

"Damn. He's going to wait for me to come back."

"Looks like it. He thinks you have the rabbit in there, remember?"

"That's right. Now I'll never get rid of him. I sure wish I had a way out of here."

Meg smiled. "You do. Glenda's car. All you have to do is help me chase Baby."

He gave her an assessing look. "With two kids in the car?"

"We're safe with you, aren't we? Besides, I can tell you anything you want to know about Lingston."

Cole just shook his head. "Hell, I guess this is the only way I'll learn what's so special about that silly rabbit."

Luke chortled, pounding on his father's back. "Silly wabbit. Silly wabbit. Silly wabbit."

Cole chuckled at his son's antics, then paused, obviously thinking. "All right." He pulled a piece of paper out of his pocket. "You have a pen?"

"Sure." She handed him one. "What are you doing?"

Cole pried Luke off his back. "I'll slip over to the station and leave Natalie a note with the station attendant that he can give to her a couple hours after we've gone. That way, she won't worry about Luke."

"Then what?"

"Then I'll sneak back over here and we'll take off west on I-10 again—after your damned rabbit."

Yes! "Oh, thank you!" Elated, Meg threw her arms around Cole and kissed him. Her enthusiasm almost knocked him over, and he caught her around the waist to steady them both.

She flushed. "Thank you," she repeated.

"You're welcome," he whispered, and gave her back a swift, hard kiss.

Her stomach turned somersaults, and her lips tingled where he'd kissed them. She inhaled sharply, and reveled in the heady aroma of musky male and warm cotton T-shirt. *Oh, my, now* this *is more like it.*

Cole released her, and she hugged that special feeling to herself as he said, "I'll be right back."

She nodded and snagged Luke as Cole crept to the edge of the car. Her gaze softened, and she looked at him with complete and utter trust.

He groaned. Closing his eyes, he said, "I have the feeling I'm going to regret this—a lot."

Meg smiled. She had a feeling she was going to enjoy this—a lot.

Chapter Three

Cole eased into traffic and tried to understand why he'd agreed to continue this crazy chase. As soon as he voiced his suspicions about the drugs, he'd realized they were ludicrous. Beau wasn't bright enough to be involved in the drug trade, and Meg was too unworldly and ingenuous. Besides, Beau hadn't had time to attach anything to the rabbit, since he'd been standing next to Cole the whole time.

That meant the suspect they were pursuing was probably just a thief. But no matter how he looked at it, this was still a dumb thing to do with a woman and two kids in the car. The only reason he was still in the chase was that he was sure the truck was long gone and they'd never catch up to it anyway.

Besides, he'd enjoyed seeing the pure joy in Meg's face when he agreed to help her. Her kiss hadn't been half-bad, either, though he didn't plan on letting her make a habit of it. She was too naive and innocent to get hooked up with the likes of him. No, he'd just go along for the ride until he learned what he needed to know about Lingston. Then, once she realized they'd never catch her rabbit, he'd take her home.

Confident now that he had a plan of action, Cole shifted into fifth gear and turned on the cruise control. The traffic had thinned out considerably on this stretch of I-10, and it was bound to stay that way for quite a while. In fact, there was nothing between here and El Paso except a few small towns and a whole lot of sand and scrub brush, enlivened only by a few scraggly mesquite bushes and the occasional roadrunner or jackrabbit.

The trip would be boring as hell if he didn't have something to occupy him. He glanced at Meg. Now there was a distraction, if he'd ever seen one. She'd unbuckled her seat belt and leaned into the back seat to referee a fight between the kids.

Her tight jeans fit snugly over what Natalie would call a pert posterior, and Cole groaned to himself as he wrenched his gaze away. He did *not* want to think about her shapely rear, even if it was pert. Hell, *especially* if it was pert. There was no place in his life for pert, perky women—even those whose impulsive kisses stirred feelings in him that he'd thought long since atrophied.

She slid back into her seat, fastening the seat belt once again. She glanced at him, and her eyes danced with mischief. Damn, there went perky again.

"They're finally quiet," he said. "What'd you do?"

"I gave 'em both a sucker. Maybe we'll have some quiet for a while."

"Good thinking. Where'd you get them?"

She waved a hand toward the floorboard. "In my purse. I keep lots of stuff in there for times like these."

He glanced at her bag. If you asked him, it was more of a suitcase than a purse. "Good grief. What all have you got in there?"

"Oh, a little bit of everything. When you're around kids as much as I am, you learn to carry things to keep them occupied."

Cole nodded. He was just now learning that himself. He glanced in the rearview mirror. Sure enough, Luke was working away with quiet concentration on the large candy bulging his cheek. Cole chuckled. "Okay, now that they're busy, tell me about Lingston."

She gave him an incredulous look. "Whatever for?"

"I'm thinking about moving there."

"Lingston? Are you crazy?"

"No, I'm serious. I've been offered the police chief's position there, and I'm thinking about taking it." Her look was incredulous, so Cole explained. "Right now, it seems like the best of the available options. Being a vice cop in San Antonio is no life for the father of a little boy."

Meg nodded. "I can see that, but wouldn't you miss San Antonio?"

Cole could tell he'd just fallen a notch in her estimation. That was just as well. That look in her eyes was only too familiar. He'd seen it in other women—thrill-seeking women who were more interested in vicariously living excitement through him than in the real Cole McKenzie.

Natalie was one of them—she'd married Cole because his profession sounded exciting and dangerous. Well, it was at times, but mostly it was just dirty and dull. When their life together didn't live up to her expectations, she'd left him—and Luke. Oh, she still loved the boy in her own way, but he just didn't fit into the new life she was trying to build.

Cole sighed. He was tired of being used that way, and he was tired of the excitement. It was best Meg learned that now. "Miss what? The gangs, the violence, the drugs?"

She grimaced. "Surely there's more to San Antonio than that."

"Sure. But that's what I see every day." He paused. "Hey, you're the one who's supposed to be answering questions, not me."

She grinned. "Well, let's make a deal. You answer questions about San Antonio, and I'll answer questions about Lingston. Okay?"

"Okay, deal. First question. You know everyone in town, right?"

"Right."

"So you know the current chief of police. Why's he leaving?"

"Amos? He's probably just bored out of his mind because nothing ever happens in that town."

Cole gave her an admonishing look.

"Okay, okay. Amos is eligible to retire, and he just became a grandfather for the third time, so he and his wife are moving to Dallas to be near the grandkids."

Cole nodded. Good. That fit in with what he knew of the man, and it meant he wasn't leaving because of the job.

"My turn now," Meg said eagerly. "What's it like being a cop in the big city?"

He'd do her a big favor if he killed any starry-eyed notions she had that his job was glamorous. "It's long, hard hours of boring scut work broken infrequently by terror-filled moments."

"But it's exciting, right?"

"Sometimes. But I can do without that kind of excitement, thank you."

Her eyes were shining with imagined thrills, so Cole tried to put a damper on her enthusiasm. "You really want to know what it's like?"

She nodded eagerly.

He leaned back and stared at the mesmerizing highway as it flashed by with monotonous regularity. "All right, picture this. Imagine hanging out in the scuzziest part of town with the dregs of humanity—people who'd cut your throat for a buck or shoot you for your boots."

She closed her eyes and nodded.

"Now imagine you're trying to catch the leader of a drug ring. Every day you get a little closer, and every day you see kids turned on to crack or heroin, but there's nothing you can do about it or you'll blow your cover."

His voice turned harsh with the memories. "Imagine you've been working your butt off in the hot, humid, stinking streets for months on end. You're just moments away from making a big bust when somehow the whole thing goes sour...and your buddy gets shot while the scum gets away scot-free."

She was quiet, so he gave her the clincher. "Now picture your son in a few years, growing up in this same environment. Imagine how *you'd* feel about all that 'excitement.'"

Cole knew his voice was tinged with bitterness, but he couldn't help it. He had to let her know how it really was.

Meg was subdued as she digested what he'd said. "I'm sorry. I didn't realize...."

He shrugged, feeling a little guilty that he'd killed her eagerness. He didn't often meet people with such a positive outlook on life, and he felt bad that he'd squelched it. "I'm sorry, too. It's not like that all the time, everywhere, but sometimes..."

She gazed at him with compassion. "That's why you want to move to Lingston."

"Right. So tell me, what's crime like in your town?"

Meg tipped her head back and quirked a smile at him. "Okay, picture this," she said, mimicking his tone. "Imagine the worst night in Lingston. You get three disturbance calls. First, the infamous Barker brothers are playing target practice with their new slingshots on the street lamps..."

She paused dramatically. "...and *you* have to take their weapons away from them. Now imagine that Sam Johnson has had too much to drink again and is wandering the neighborhood, and you have to haul him in to sleep it off. And imagine, just when you're moments away from calling it a night, you get an irate call saying that Betsy Conolly's goat is eating Mrs. Jenkins's pansies—*again*."

She widened her eyes and clasped her hands at her throat. "Imagine how *you'd* feel with all that 'excitement.'"

He chuckled. He was glad to see he hadn't totally subdued her spirits. "Sounds good to me. Is that an accurate portrayal?"

"Very accurate—"

"Daddy, me *thirsty*," declared Luke from the back seat.

"Me too," said Susie.

Cole glanced back at them and grimaced. Somehow, they'd managed to smear the suckers all over themselves. Luke was coated in orange and Susie in red. He sighed. How children could manage to get so messy when they weren't even doing anything amazed him.

He gave Meg a speculative look. "I don't suppose you have any water in that bag of yours, do you?"

She shook her head.

"That's what I was afraid of." He raised his voice to answer Luke. "Okay, sport. Next exit, we'll get you something to drink." He glanced down at the dash. "Sorry for the delay, Meg, but we need gas anyway."

She nodded, and he pulled off the highway and into the nearest gas station. Meg insisted on paying, since it was her rabbit they were chasing, so he pumped the gas while she hurried inside to pay and get the children something to drink.

When she returned, he glanced at her over the hood of the car. "All set?"

She nodded and started to crawl in, but Luke was in her seat. "C'mon, Luke, get in the back—" She broke off, and a horrified look came over her face. "My Lord, what is that smell?"

Cole opened the door, took one sniff and identified it. "Mace."

"It smells worse than skunk."

"Daddy, me need dwink," Luke declared, his face screwed up in a comical expression that showed he was trying hard not to breathe in the acrid aroma.

"Luke, what did you do?" Cole asked.

"Nothin'."

Cole glanced around for the source of the odor. There was nothing obvious in sight, so he opened the glove compartment and the stench came rolling out, along with a silver can of tear gas. He shut it quickly. "All right, everybody out. We've got to get this smell out of here before we get moving again."

The kids scrambled out, and Meg herded them over to the side of the station. Cole parked next to them, then opened all the doors and windows. Sighing in exasperation, he walked over to look down at the two children, who were drinking their sodas.

"Okay," he said in an ominous tone. "What happened?"

Luke kept his eyes downcast, but Susie piped up. "He thought it would smell good, so he spwayed it."

Luke glared at her and swung his arm in her direction, as if to negate what she'd said. "No, me dint."

"Did too."

"Not."

Meg intervened. "All right, that's enough. Just finish your drinks, and we'll get you guys cleaned up, okay?"

Luke just kept his eyes downcast, but Susie looked up at the adults with a confiding expression. "He lies, you know."

It was all Cole could do to keep from laughing out loud. He caught Meg's gaze, and they shared an amused glance.

Meg's breath caught in her throat. It was the kind of warm, intimate moment married couples shared—and it scared the hell out of her. Damn Cole McKenzie, anyway. One moment he acted like Steven Seagal and the next like Tom Hanks. It was enough to drive any woman crazy.

Oh, she could deal with either type, but when he switched back and forth like that, it kept her off balance, and she didn't quite know how to handle it.

She jerked her gaze away from his. "All right, Susie, let's get you cleaned up. Cole will take care of Luke." They were losing time, but since they couldn't get back into the car until it had aired out, they might as well get the kids clean.

She ushered the little girl into the ladies' room and wet a paper towel so she could clean the candy from her face and hands. "Good grief, Susie, how'd you get it in your hair?"

Meg was glad of the distraction—she couldn't let the Tom Hankses of this world seduce her with their safety and security, and the promise of sweet little children. No, she was going to find herself a Steven Seagal and add a little spice and danger to her life—just as soon as she found her rabbit.

Once the little girl was clean, Meg went outside and found Cole and his son standing next to the car. Luke looked downright mutinous, with his chubby arms crossed and a heavy frown on his face. Uh-oh. What was this about?

Cole urged the boy forward. "Go on, Luke."

Luke just shook his head and scowled even harder.

"Tell Meg you're sorry."

Luke muttered something Meg didn't catch.

"What was that?" Cole's voice was hard, uncompromising.

Luke turned a beady eye on his father. "Me sowwy!"

Cole looked as though he were going to force the boy to repeat it, but Meg stifled a chuckle and spoke up. "Thank you, Luke."

Luke's pout abated a little as he gave her a speculative look, obviously trying to figure out whether she was one of the good guys.

"What else, Luke?" Cole said. When Luke did nothing but shake his head, Cole turned to Meg. "Since it's your car—or rather your cousin's car—we decided you should determine what Luke's punishment is."

No wonder Luke was staring at her as though she were a monster. Meg bit her lip and thought. Susie watched in awed fascination, obviously wondering what awful thing Meg was going to do to him. It seemed the poor kid had already gotten a royal chewing-out by his father. That was punishment enough for a boy his age.

She knelt in front of Luke so that she could look him in the eye. When he gave her a wary look, Meg said, "Did you make that bad smell on purpose, Luke?"

He shook his head, his face still mutinous.

"Are you really sorry for what you did?"

He looked at her then, his face dawning with innocent hope, and nodded.

"And you're never going to do it again?"

This time he shook his head in an emphatic no.

Thankfully, Cole kept quiet and let her deal with this in her own way. It was the least he could do after dumping this situation on her in the first place.

She sighed heavily. "All right, this is going to hurt me more than it's going to hurt you. I think your punishment should be . . . a kiss."

A slow smile spread across Luke's face.

"Does that sound okay to you?"

He nodded shyly.

"All right, then, let's get it over with." She scrunched her face up as if she were in pain and pointed to her cheek. "Put it right there, pardner."

Giggling, Luke gave her a swift peck where she'd indicated.

"Whew," Meg exclaimed. "I'm glad that's over. Can we get moving again now?"

Luke nodded, then threw his arms around her neck. "Go now."

She chuckled and hugged the little boy, catching a tender expression on Cole's face.

Uh-oh, it was Tom Hanks again. She didn't need this—she had enough people to take care of. And speaking of that . . . Meg had something else she had to do before they could resume the chase. "Uh, can you wait a minute? I just remembered I have to make a phone call."

"Sure—I'll just get the kids settled in."

"Susie's toys are probably in the trunk. That might help."

Cole nodded and turned to open the trunk while Meg called home.

"Hi, Pops, it's Meg."

"Meg? Where are you?"

Where did he think she was? He knew she'd planned on staying the weekend in San Antonio. She ignored his question, not wanting to worry him. "Did you take your medicine?"

"Medicine?"

Meg sighed. He was hopeless sometimes. "Yes, your medicine. I left it out on the counter for you. Go take one right now, okay, Pops?"

"Are you all right?"

"Yes, I'm fine."

"Are you sure?"

Good grief, what was wrong with him? "I'll be fine if you'll just take your medicine."

"Oh, all right," he grumbled. "But you call if you need anything, you hear?"

"All right, I will. Bye now, Pops. I love you."

Shaking her head, Meg hung up the phone. He sure sounded distracted—she just hoped he'd take his pill.

Cole drove up to the phone booth. "Ready?"

Meg nodded. Though the car hadn't had time to completely air out, the smell was bearable now. She got in, and they headed off again.

As he pulled back on the highway, he turned to her with a heart-melting smile. "Thanks," he said softly.

"For what?" She knew her voice sounded defensive, but she couldn't help it. She knew what was coming, and she didn't want to hear it. She'd seen that expression on men's faces before—mostly widowers who looked at her as though she'd be the perfect mother for their children.

"For taking the time to treat Luke so nice."

She shrugged. "It was nothing."

"No. It was something. I know you're in a hurry to catch up to your truck. Luke's prank slowed you down. You were well within your rights to be angry with him, but you treated him with respect. You're good with kids."

Yeah, just as she'd expected. Good with kids. She could see the epitaph on her tombstone now. *Here lies Dependable Old Meg, Spinster. She never made love, but she was good with children and rabbits.*

Damn, why couldn't someone just once compliment her on something impractical—like her looks or her body? All her life she'd been dying for someone to tell her she was sexy, or provocative, or just plain pretty. But no, she was "good with kids." She sighed.

"Did I say something wrong?"

"No, no. It's okay—it's easy to be nice to him. You have a great son there."

"Yeah," Luke said from the back seat. "Grrrrrreat!"

Cole laughed. "Modest, too. You see now why I want to move to Lingston?"

Meg shook her head. "Not really. I understand the horrors of your job, but not all of San Antonio is like that, surely. Other people raise their children there."

Cole turned serious as he stared down the highway. "Maybe. But I want to spend more time with my son. I want him to have a happy, safe childhood. I want the best for him."

"And you think that's Lingston?"

"Maybe. That's what you're supposed to help me find out."

If Cole was that determined, then there was no way she was going to stop him from learning what he wanted to know. She might as well help him. She sighed. "Okay, what do you want to know?"

For the next hour, she answered endless questions about Lingston's school system, its crime rate, its politics, its medical facilities, and all of the town's amenities. To every question, Meg gave a complete and honest answer—all dull and dry. That didn't seem to bother Cole, though. In fact, he looked downright pleased.

Finally, a welcome distraction came from the back seat when Luke and Susie got into a fight, arms flailing as they tried to hit each other. Luckily, they missed, belted in as they were on opposite sides of the car.

"What's going on back there?" Cole asked in a stern voice.

"She started it."

"Did not."

"Did too."

Meg leaned between the seats to see what was going on. "Whoa, kids. Tell me what's wrong."

Luke scowled. "She took my bear."

"No!" Susie yelled. "It's *my* bear."

"*My* turn."

Meg sighed. "Susie, you know Luke doesn't have any toys with him and you have to share. You have your doll, and you can't give both of them the attention they need, so let Luke have the bear, okay?"

Susie nodded reluctantly and passed the bear over to Luke, who snatched it and hugged it to his chest.

"What do you say, Luke?" Cole asked.

"T'ank you."

Meg smiled at him. He was a good kid. Luke returned her smile with a heartwarming one of his own, a perfect copy of his father's.

"Aunt Meg?" Susie asked. Meg wasn't her aunt, but Susie wasn't old enough yet to grasp the cousin relationship, so they'd settled on *aunt*. "I gotta go potty."

Predictably, Luke echoed her. "Me too."

"All right. I'll see what I can do." Meg slid back into her seat and muttered, "If it isn't one thing, it's another." Once again, it would slow down the chase, but the children's needs came first.

Cole chuckled. "There's a rest area up ahead. We can stop there."

"Good."

Cole gave her another one of those "You're good with kids" smiles and pulled off into the deserted rest area. Meg tried to ignore him as she waited to get out of the car. She just wanted to get this chase over with,

retrieve her rabbit, win the bet, then get on with finding a man who wanted her for herself—not to play
mommy to his kids.

"Okay, Susie," Meg said. "Let's go to the bathroom."

"Me too," Luke said.

Surprised, Meg said, "Don't you want to go with
your daddy?"

"No. Go wif you."

She looked at Cole, but he just shrugged. "He
doesn't see much of his mother."

Meg nodded. The poor little guy probably just
wanted some attention from a woman for a change.
"Okay, let's go."

The children had been cooped up in the car for so
long that they let out some of their excess energy by
running whooping toward the bathrooms like wild
animals. Meg followed at a more leisurely pace.

Once Luke and Susie finished using the bathroom,
they started to run out, but Meg halted them. Just because she wasn't their mother, that didn't mean she
wouldn't make sure they behaved properly. "Wait a
minute, kiddos. You forgot to wash your hands."

"Do we hafta?" Susie whined.

"Yes, you have to. Come on, now. Luke first."

Meg raised him to the sink and started to turn on the
water, but he said, "No, no, me do it."

Knowing how important it was for three-year-olds
to do everything for themselves, she held the little boy
while he carefully pumped pink liquid soap into his
hand.

Concentrating hard, Luke pushed the plunger in with meticulous attention. After he'd repeated the action five slooooow times, Susie became impatient. "You're gonna use it all up," she complained.

"Am not," he declared, and pushed the button twice more, until his small hand was overflowing with soap.

"Are too." Susie reached up as if to snatch some of it away from him, and Luke jerked his hand back, smacking Meg in the forehead with a handful of the gooey pink liquid.

"Ow!" Meg said. That hurt. It didn't taste too good, either. Even now, the soap dribbled over one eye and down across her cheek to the corner of her mouth.

Squinting at Luke with one eye closed, she made out a look of horror on his face. Poor kid—he probably thought he was going to get spanked.

She set the boy down, then wiped the soap out of her eye. "This means war," she declared, and tackled him, tickling him with one hand while she smeared soap all over his hands and arms with the other. "See how you like it."

Luke chortled with glee, and Susie leaped around, shrieking with laughter as she joined in the fray.

"Hey, what's going on here?" Cole's deep voice reverberated throughout the bathroom, and they looked up guiltily, all three dripping with pink soap.

Cole stood there with his arms crossed. His stern expression was marred somewhat by the twitch at the corner of his mouth. Lord, how embarrassing to have him standing there looking so gorgeous while she was an utter mess. The soap was everywhere—on her face, her arms, her blouse, even in her hair. Well, there was nothing to do but brazen it out.

Meg pouted, pointing at Luke. "He started it."

Luke and Susie giggled, and Cole gave a startled laugh. Turning to the children, he asked, "Is that true?"

"No, she did it, she did it!" they squealed, laughing and pointing at Meg.

"Well," Cole said, obviously fighting to keep a straight face, "I guess you're outnumbered, Meg. Let's get you all cleaned up, then we'll think of a suitable punishment."

He helped the giggling children get rid of the soap while Meg cleaned up as best she could. It wasn't great. She still looked wet and bedraggled and definitely unsexy, but it would have to do.

Once they were finished, Cole said, "Okay, Meg, time to take your punishment. What's it gonna be?"

"A kiss, a kiss!" shouted the kids, jumping up and down in delight.

Meg's heart turned over in her chest. Oh, no. Not now. Not when she looked like *this*.

Cole just grinned, with a devilish twinkle in his eye. "All right, but this is going to hurt me more than it does you." He screwed up his face in a comical imitation of her earlier expression and pointed to his cheek. "Plant it right there, pardner."

The children were giggling, so Meg did the only thing she could. She pursed her lips, intending to give his cheek the merest brush of her lips, but when she stepped toward him, her foot skidded on some of the spilled soap and she stumbled.

She grabbed his shoulders for support, and he gave her a surprised look as he caught her around the waist. Meg tried hard to remember how to breathe, but with his arms around her and his hard-muscled chest plastered against hers, it was very difficult.

Feeling some explanation was necessary, she said, "I slipped."

"I noticed," he whispered. "But you forgot something."

"What?"

"The kiss." His lips were just a breath away as he smiled wickedly, giving her a searching look with his eyes half-lidded and his gaze dangerously seductive.

"Oh, my," she breathed, just before his lips claimed hers.

The kiss was everything she'd ever dreamed of—soft at first, then hard and searching as she responded to his probing. She twined her arms around his neck, and her pulse beat in excitement. Here was her bad-boy lover at last. No more widowers with children for her—she'd take this sexy, exciting cop any time.

An insistent tugging distracted her, and she glanced dazedly down at the source of the sensation. It was Luke, pulling at her pant leg.

As she remained weak-kneed in his father's arms, the boy grinned up at her. "You my other mommy now?"

Chapter Four

Beau paced beside his car. It'd been two hours since he'd spotted Cole's car from the interstate, and the station attendant wouldn't let him near it. Now there was nothing to do but wait...wait for Natty's ex-husband to return, and wait to get that blasted bunny.

What an afternoon. This wasn't exactly the way he'd planned to spend the day he proposed to Natty. All his romantic plans were shot to hell. He cast a covetous glance at Cole's car. If he could just get into it and get that ring, he might be able to redeem at least part of the day.

He shot a glance at Natty. She was a little miffed at him because he hadn't said anything when he saw her kid sneaking into Cole's car. Hell, the kid was all right with his father, wasn't he? Her anger didn't show, though. She appeared cool and comfortable sitting in the car, like she didn't have a care in the world.

Normally, he adored that aspect of her, but right now it just served to remind him how uncomfortable he was. Though it was October, he was still sweltering. He'd taken off his tuxedo jacket and the tie, but the starched shirt itched enough to drive him crazy.

Beau glanced up as the station attendant approached Natty. The man glanced at his watch, then pulled a piece of paper out of his shirt pocket. "Here," he said, thrusting his grease-covered hand at her. "This is for you."

Natty took it and thanked him.

Beau frowned at the man. "What's that?"

"A note." He jerked a thumb at Cole's car. "That guy asked me to give it to her."

Beau felt his temper rise. "You mean you've had the note all this time...and you didn't give it to us? Why not?"

The man shrugged and grinned. "He asked me to wait a couple of hours."

"He asked you to— And you—" Beau's fury left him incoherent. It was obvious the man had enjoyed watching Beau pace and fume while he had that note in his pocket the whole time. Beau glared at him, and the man had the insolence to widen his grin even more, then turn and saunter off.

"Beau?" Natty said.

"What?" he snapped.

Natty gave him a startled look, and he remembered that this was the woman he loved. He shouldn't take out his anger on her. Beau took a deep breath and moderated his tone. "I'm sorry, darling, what is it?"

Natty held out the note. "Lukie's all right."

He snatched the note out of her hand and read it.

Natalie, Luke sneaked into my car while we were stopped. Don't worry, he's fine. We're still following the truck and will call you from El Paso when we stop for the night, Cole.

Beau clenched the note in his fist. "But what about the *bunny?*"

Natty looked at him as though he were crazy. "The bunny?"

Beau controlled his temper with an effort. This was his future wife he was talking to. "Remember, I have to get that ring back or I'll lose my job."

"That's right, I'd forgotten." Her voice sounded concerned, so Beau gave her a fond smile.

"Well, Cole said earlier that it's in the truck he's chasing," Natty ventured.

Beau snorted in disbelief. "That's not what the kid said—he said it's in the car."

Natty arched a well-shaped eyebrow at him. "Well, I hate to break it to you, Beau, but children don't always tell the truth."

"You mean he lied to me?"

"I mean it's possible he told *us* a fib. You were being so rotten—"

"Hell, Natty, I didn't mean it. I was just worried about my job."

"I know that, but Lukie didn't. Since you were being so mean, he probably fibbed so he could go back to his daddy."

Damn. That changed everything. "So the bunny could be anywhere."

"Yes, but it's possible he did drop it in Cole's car. It's either there...or they have it with them...or maybe it really is in the truck."

"Good point." He glanced at the stall. "But first things first. How are we going to search that car?" He knew the attendant wouldn't let him anywhere near it.

Natty smiled and waved the note at him. "Let me handle it—you stay here."

Beau slumped against his car and watched as Natty approached the man and showed him the note. Soon she was searching the car. Beau started over to help her, but she shook her head at him, so he stayed where he was and fretted.

Well, at least she seemed to be doing a thorough job of it. Eventually she shut the car door and spoke to the attendant, then came back empty-handed.

"Not there?"

"No, it's not there. I looked everywhere."

Curious, Beau asked, "How'd you get him to let you search it?"

She smiled. "I just showed him the note and told him I was concerned that my son had left his favorite toy in the car. He even told me what Cole was driving when he left—a blue Camry."

Yeah, well, if Natty turned that smile on him, Beau would do anything she asked, too. He sighed. "Okay, it's not in the car, so it's either with your kid or it's in the truck. In either case, we need to follow them to El Paso."

Natty looked at him like she thought he was crazy. "You've got to be kidding. They have a two-hour head start on us."

"I know, but my car is faster than his, and I've got a radar detector. We'll catch them, don't worry. Come on, get in."

Natty gave him a doubtful look, but climbed in anyway. "All right, but this ring you bought me better be worth it."

COLE had just barely registered Luke's question when Meg jerked out of his arms.

"Mommy?" she squeaked in a horrified voice. She backed away, then darted an alarmed look at Cole and fled the bathroom.

Now what was that all about? Here they'd been enjoying a perfectly nice kiss—at least he had. No, damn it, she had, too. Her eager response had sure felt that way to him. Why would his son's innocent question send her running off like a scared rabbit?

He glanced down at Luke and Susie. If their expressions were any indication, they were just as confused.

"Daddy?"

"Yes, Luke?"

"She mad?"

Susie scowled and placed her chubby hands on her hips. "Not your mommy. *My* Aunt Meg."

Luke's face turned mutinous, and Cole intervened before another fight could erupt.

Kneeling down to stare Luke in the eye, Cole said, "That's right, Luke. Meg's not mommy."

"Not *like* me?" Luke asked, his face screwed up as if he were going to start crying any minute.

Cole's heart twisted. *How could anyone not like Luke?* "Of course she likes you, sport. It's just that Meg knows you already have a mother. You understand?"

Luke nodded reluctantly.

Susie grinned in triumph. "See? *My* Aunt Meg."

Luke's bottom lip quivered. Poor kid. He must really miss a woman's influence. "Maybe Meg will be your aunt, too," Cole said. "Would you like to ask her?"

Luke's eyes brightened, but Susie scowled. She obviously didn't want to give up her advantage. Quickly Cole added, "And I can be Susie's uncle Cole."

The sullen expressions disappeared from both kids' faces, and they looked up at Cole with interest.

"Okay," Susie said with a giggle.

Luke tugged on his hand. "C'mon."

They exited the bathroom and found Meg standing near a picnic table, her arms wrapped around her slender body, staring into the sunset.

As they approached, Meg whirled around to give Cole a look of apprehension and defiance. Luke's question must have spooked her, but Cole wasn't sure whether it was the thought of being Luke's mother—or the idea of being Cole's wife.

If it was the latter, well, hell, he hadn't even asked her. It was only a kiss, for heaven's sake. He couldn't help it if his three-year-old son had interpreted it incorrectly.

The kids came to a stop and looked up at the adults. "Ask her, Daddy," Luke said in a loud whisper.

The uneasy look on Meg's face deepened, and Cole toyed with the idea of getting down on one knee, just to see how she'd react. He curbed the impulse, doubting she'd find it amusing.

He let her off the hook. "Luke understands you're not his mother, but if it's all right with you, he'd like you to be his aunt."

The apprehension faded from Meg's face as she gave the boy a smile. "Thank you, Luke. I'd love to be your aunt Meg."

Susie piped up. "And he's my uncle Cole."

Everyone beamed at each other, happy with their new relationships. Everyone but Cole.

If Meg was Luke's aunt, that made her...his sister. He didn't care for that thought at all, especially after experiencing one of her kisses. How about stepsister? Or sister-in-law? That was better—no blood relation at all.

Satisfied, Cole decided he'd better set things straight, or he wouldn't get anywhere with his new relative. "Listen. What happened back there in the bathroom..."

Meg shrugged but wouldn't meet his eyes. "No big deal. I'm sorry I ran. It's just..." She spread her hands helplessly, unwilling—or unable—to put her anxiety into words.

"Look, I didn't mean—"

"It's okay." Meg looked embarrassed. "I know you didn't. It's me. I'm just leery of single men with children. Too many of them want me to be—" She broke off and bit her lip, obviously regretting having said too much.

Cole chuckled, and Meg looked at him in bewilderment. He grinned. "I was just wondering if either of us was capable of finishing a sentence."

She grinned back. "You just did. Come to think of it, so did I."

Good—the sparkle was back in her eyes, and she'd stopped treating him as though he had leprosy. As he wondered how to take advantage of their newfound relationship, a whimpering sound caught his attention.

Cole glanced down. What was it? He spotted a small furry shape and groaned.

Luke's face lit up. "Look, Daddy—a puppy."

Yes, it was definitely a puppy. A dirty, bedraggled mongrel of a dog who looked up at them with soulful eyes.

Luke started to run to the dog, but Cole caught him around the waist. "Whoa, hold on there, sport. You don't know if it's friendly or not."

No such inhibitions curbed Meg. Kneeling next to the dog, she said, "Don't be ridiculous. It's just a puppy." The dog wagged its tail and licked her hand. "See?"

That was all the encouragement Luke and Susie needed. They darted over to the dog, prepared to hug it to death, but Meg restrained them, showing them how to pet it without scaring the life out of the poor mutt.

Luke turned a joyous face up to his father. "Daddy, me keep?"

Ah, hell, he'd seen this coming. "No, Luke. Absolutely not. I told you we can't have a dog in our apartment."

Luke's face fell, but Cole stood firm. This was *not* going to be a small dog when it grew up. It had the facial markings of a German Shepherd, the coloring and bushy tail of a Collie and the floppy ears of a Labrador—a true Heinz 57. "Its owners must be around somewhere. We'll just have to find them."

"I don't think so," Meg said.

"What?"

"Look around. The place is deserted except for us. I don't think this puppy belongs to anyone anymore." She examined it. "*She* doesn't have a collar, and it looks as though she hasn't been fed in quite a while either. She's probably thirsty, too. Let's get her something to drink." She gathered the dog up in her arms and carried her to the bathroom.

Cole had no choice but to follow and watch as Meg filled a sink. The pup put her clumsy paws in the water and lapped it up eagerly. Cole had to admit that Meg was right. The dog had been abandoned.

Once the puppy finished slaking her thirst, she joyously licked every part of Meg she could reach. When Luke and Susie moved closer to see what was going on, the wet dog wriggled and squirmed so that she could lick their faces, as well. Luke squealed in delight, and Cole frowned. Luke was already becoming attached to the dog.

"Daddy, please?"

Cole repeated himself. "We can't keep a dog in an apartment."

"But if you're moving to Lingston, you'll have a house, not an apartment," Meg pointed out.

"I haven't decided yet if I'm moving to Lingston or not." Actually, Cole had already decided Lingston was just the place to raise his son, but he didn't like being browbeaten into taking this dog. *He* would make the decisions in this family—not Luke, and certainly not Meg. "Besides, dogs are too much responsibility for a three-year-old to handle."

"So you want to leave the poor thing here to starve to death?"

"If you're so worried about the dog, then *you* take it."

"Well, then, I will. Or I'll find a good home for her. But first things first. We have to take her with us and find her something to eat."

Cole scowled. He'd been outmaneuvered. He didn't want to take the dog, but he couldn't leave it here, either. Even if he wanted to, Meg wouldn't let him.

The puppy whimpered and licked Meg's face, basically managing to look pitiful. Four pairs of eyes turned in unison to stare up at him beseechingly: Meg's, Luke's, Susie's—and the damned dog's.

Hell. "All right, we'll take her with us." He gave Luke a stern look. "But we are *not* keeping this dog, you understand?"

"'Kay," Luke said, as an expression of joy suffused his face.

So why do I have the distinct feeling I've just been had?

MEG GLANCED UP from the map. "Fort Stockton is just ahead. We can pull off there and get something to eat."

Cole conceded the necessity, since it was time for the kids to eat dinner anyway, but he was *not* going to let some stray animal run his life. He didn't know how he'd let himself be talked into going on this rabbit chase with a woman, two kids and a dog, but he did know he had to get back some measure of control.

Starting now.

"All right, but I'm *not* searching through a strange town to find puppy food. The dog can eat people food and like it."

"Okay," Meg said, taking some of the satisfaction out of his belligerence. "There's a diner over there on the right, just off the interstate."

Cole grunted at her acknowledgment and pulled into the parking lot.

"C'mon, Lady," Luke said. "Time to eat."

Terrific. Luke had given the dog a name already. Now they'd never get rid of it. And what a name. Lady... for this mongrel? Tramp was more like it. Irritated, Cole snapped, "You can't take the dog into the restaurant."

Luke gave him a stricken look. "But Lady hungwy."

"I know, sport, but dogs aren't allowed in restaurants." Cole was more confident now—he had the law on his side. "You'll just have to leave her in the car, and we'll bring her something after we finish."

Luke's lower lip protruded, and he began to wail. "Don't wanna!"

That set Susie off, and she began crying, too.

Now what was he supposed to do? Cole glanced at Meg for help. He'd be more than willing to relinquish control for the moment, if she could just get the kids to stop crying.

Meg gave him an amused look. "There's a hamburger place across the road, with tables outside. Why don't we eat there, so Lady can join us? How does that sound, Luke?"

Luke's tears dried up, and Cole gave Meg an admiring glance. He should have thought of that himself. Too bad Meg didn't like to play mom—he could probably learn a lot from her.

They parked at the fast-food restaurant, and Cole went inside to place their order while Meg took the kids to wash their hands. As he waited for the food, he thought about the strange set of contradictions that made up Meg Hollingsworth. The woman was a soft touch when it came to kids and animals, but she craved the excitement and thrills of the big city. The two didn't mesh. Just which was the real Meg, anyway?

He picked up their dinner and walked out to the table, then frowned when he saw Meg trying to herd the energetic puppy to the table.

"Wait here," he said. "I saw some rope in the trunk earlier. I'll make a leash so we don't have to worry about her running off while we eat."

Good grief, what was he saying? He wanted to get rid of the dog, didn't he? Sure, but he didn't want to be responsible for it getting run over—and there was a lot of traffic on this road. Too much for this dumb mutt to avoid.

"Good idea," Meg said as she foiled another getaway attempt.

Cole grimaced to himself as he cut the rope and fastened it around the dog's neck. He had the sinking feeling that he was going to end up taking care of this dog, no matter what anyone promised.

Once the leash was fastened, the puppy's nose worked overtime as she caught the scent of food. She wriggled free, then bounded over to the table. Once there, she stopped to stare up at Luke with hope-filled eyes, her plumed tail wagging so much it raised a cloud of dust.

Smart dog—she knew who the soft touch was right away. Cole tied the rope to the bench and joined them at the table, watching as Meg assumed the job of making sure Luke and Susie ate while Lady didn't get overfed because of the children's generosity.

Now that the kids were occupied, Cole was more curious than ever about Meg's apparent contradictions. "So tell me more about your life in Lingston."

She rolled her eyes. "Haven't you heard enough yet?"

"This time I'm not asking about the town—I'm asking about you."

"Me? Why?" Her expression turned wary.

He shrugged. "Why not? We've got lots of time to kill while we chase after this rabbit of yours, and the kids aren't exactly scintillating conversationalists. What else is there to do? Play road games?"

She grinned. "True. What do you want to know?"

"What do you do for fun?"

It was her turn to shrug. "I don't have much time for play. I have to sneak it in between baby-sitting jobs, taking care of the rabbits and civic activities." She paused. "They're fun, I guess—some of them."

That wasn't how "dependable old Meg" had described them earlier. "But what about you? When you have time for yourself, what do you enjoy doing?"

"I read, remember?"

That was right—romance novels. Was that where she'd gotten her strange ideas? Hoping for some insight into her character, Cole asked, "What is it you like about reading?"

Her eyes turned distant as she contemplated his question. "Oh, in books I can go anywhere, to any time period, and be somebody else. I can be a courtesan in ancient Rome, or a stockbroker in New York, or...fly ships to Venus. I can go places I've never been, see things I've never seen—all without leaving my room." Her voice faltered on the last sentence.

"I get the feeling you'd rather experience some of those things firsthand, instead of vicariously."

"Of course. Wouldn't you?" She shook her head. "No, I guess you wouldn't. I forgot. You're Mr. I-Don't-Like-Excitement McKenzie."

He raised an eyebrow. So she had him pegged as a stick-in-the-mud, did she? Well, better that than have her hanging all over him like a thrill junkie. "And you think you'll be able to do that if you move to San Antonio?"

"It's got to be better than Lingston."

"In what way?"

"Oh, the excitement of the River Walk—nightclubs, dancing, parties..."

"Drunks, pushers, rapists..."

She shot him a dirty look. "Has anyone ever told you you're a cynic?"

"I'm not a cynic. I'm a realist." He sighed. "Okay, so it's not like that everywhere. You just have to be careful if you want to be a party animal...if that's what you really want?"

Meg looked wistful. "Yeah, I guess so."

"It loses something after a while, you know."

She gave him a doubtful look. "Well, maybe, but I'd sure like to find out for myself."

He decided to take another tack. "So what happens if we find Baby and you win the bet? What about your brother and grandfather?"

She waved his question away as if it were immaterial. "Oh, they'll love San Antonio once they get used to it."

"What'll they do there?"

"If Pops sells the farm, he'll have enough money so he won't have to work anymore—and Jerry can get a job," she added defensively. "I will, too."

"Do you really think they'll be happy there?"

"Of course they will. Besides, I've put up with the rabbit farm for years. Isn't it time they did what I want for a change?" She looked guilty, and Cole realized she really did care for her family. Too bad they didn't seem to return the sentiment.

And without anyone to watch out for her, there were many in the city who would be only too willing to take advantage of an innocent like her. The life would probably make her miserable, but there was no use in telling her that. She'd never believe him until she experienced it for herself.

And if she did, there was a chance she'd get hooked on the thrills of courting danger. It was a scenario Cole had seen all too often, and he didn't want it to happen to Meg.

Of course, the easiest way to do that was to make sure they never retrieved that rabbit. That was a foregone conclusion since the thief was undoubtedly long gone by now, but no matter. Cole would use the time he had to convince Meg the partying life wasn't for her.

"I'm not sure I'd feel comfortable making that decision for *my* family," he said softly.

"What do you know about it? The only one you have to worry about is Luke—and he's too young to make decisions for himself."

He raised an amused eyebrow. "Luke isn't my only family, you know. I have parents like everyone else— even sisters and brothers."

"Oh, of course. I just never thought..." She glanced at him with sympathy-filled eyes. "Did you have a bad home life?"

"No, actually, it was a wonderful home life. With six kids, life was never dull at the McKenzie house."

"Oh? Why not?"

"We all came pretty much a year and a half apart, so we're close—Mom made sure of that. She always dispensed love, cookies and justice with an even hand, and made sure the house was filled with joy and laughter."

Meg's eyes turned wistful. "Sounds wonderful."

This from a woman who claimed to want the fast life? Cole grinned. "Yes, it was, except when you have three older sisters and you want to use the bathroom.

Sometimes I think I spent my entire childhood waiting outside a closed door with my legs crossed.''

Meg grinned. ''I can see where that might be a problem.''

''And since I'm the youngest, my older brothers always ganged up on me, and my sisters mothered me so much that I had no peace.''

''Yeah, right. I'll bet you were spoiled rotten.''

He laughed out loud. ''That, too, I guess. But my family wouldn't let me get too spoiled. They love nothing more than taking me down a peg.''

''I still think it sounds wonderful.''

Cole suppressed a smile at the wistful tone in her voice. Luke wasn't the only one starved for affection. What must it have been like to grow up as she did, with only a busy grandfather and a younger brother to meet the needs of an affection-starved teenager? Cole couldn't imagine a life without his large, boisterous family. No wonder she craved something different.

''It's exciting—I'll give you that. You never know what's going to happen next, especially when all the aunts, uncles and cousins get together. Lord, what a madhouse.''

''What about your father? What does he do?''

''He's a cop like me. It's sort of a family tradition—my two brothers are on the force, too, as well as one of my sisters.''

''Really? So why do you want to move away from them?''

''My family lives in Austin, not San Antone.''

Meg gazed at him thoughtfully. ''And Lingston is a lot closer to Austin.''

"There's that, too," he admitted. "I moved to San Antonio because Natalie wanted to, plus I wanted to get more involved with the war on crime—to be where the action was. Boy, did I get my wish."

I knew it, Meg thought. To be where the action was? That was a yen for excitement if she'd ever heard of one. There was a little of the bad boy in him yet, she'd bet on it.

Cole rose to clear the mess off the table. "Well, we'd better get going or we'll never find your rabbit."

Meg stood to help him. "Do you think we still have a chance of catching him?" With the delays the children and dog had caused, she wasn't at all sure of that.

"Maybe." Cole's voice sounded doubtful. "He doesn't know he's being followed, so maybe he's taking it easy. If so, there's a chance we can catch him— if he's still on the interstate. Why don't we drive as far as El Paso tonight? Then, if we don't find him on the way, we'll make other plans."

It sounded reasonable. "Okay. I'll just get the kids cleaned up—and you can walk the dog."

Cole looked down at the puppy with a pained expression on his face. "Walk the dog. Great. Somehow I knew I'd end up taking care of the mutt."

Meg grinned. "It's only for a few minutes. Unless you'd rather take care of the kids?"

Cole shook his head. "No, that's okay. You're better at that than I am. I'll just stay here and take care of... Lady."

As she cleaned up the kids, Meg's thoughts drifted to Cole. He wasn't *totally* the Tom Hanks type, but he wasn't Steven Seagal either. Maybe this could work to her advantage. If she played her cards right, she might coax Steven out to play but leave caring Tom in charge of the aftermath.

The thought made her tingle with excitement. Yes, this had definite possibilities. Could she do it?

Meg nodded decisively. Yes, she could. She'd gone looking for danger and thrills, and this might be her last chance to get them. If they didn't catch up to Baby by the time they reached El Paso, then her bet was lost, and with it, all chance of a life in San Antonio.

She made herself a promise. If that happened, then she'd just have to make the most of the little adventure she was having right now—with Cole.

She steered the kids out of the bathroom, and her heart skipped a beat as she gazed at Cole. My, my, he was gorgeous. He still resembled the brooding hero of her imagination, especially the way he looked in his tight jeans and T-shirt, with his dark hair tousled by the wind, squinting into the night.

The thought sent a flush of sweet longing through her, and she wondered what it would be like to make love to a man. No, not to any man. She wondered what it would be like to make love to Cole.

She stared, spellbound, and began weaving a fantasy around the two of them. His kiss had been wonderfully gentle, with a hint of passion held barely in check. What would it be like to unleash that passion? To see it turned on her?

She swallowed hard. She didn't know, but she sure wanted to find out. *Just how do you go about seducing a man, anyway?*

''Meg?'' Cole said in a tentative voice.

Oh, no. She'd been caught leering at him. She blushed and turned away, pretending to watch the traffic on the interstate. "Looks like we'd better get going, huh?"

"Yeah, I—"

She gave a sudden start of surprise. "I don't believe it."

"What is it?"

"I thought I saw— No, it couldn't be."

"Saw what?"

"A white sports car— It looked just like Beau's, and it had a man and a woman riding in it. Do you think—?"

They glanced at each other and shook their heads simultaneously. "Naw," Cole said.

Chapter Five

Beau drove past the exit sign for Fort Stockton and cursed his own stupidity. He should have caught up to Cole by now, but his prospects were looking worse with each mile that passed. How could he have mixed up those rings?

"Beau, can't we stop?" Natalie whined. "I'm getting hungry."

Irritation flashed through him. She had no sympathy for what *he* was going through—all she could think about was herself. "We can't stop—we can't afford to waste the time."

"Surely a few minutes wouldn't hurt. I've got to get something to eat, or I'll be sick." A thread of steel entered her voice. "You wouldn't want me to get sick in your nice new car, would you?"

She had a point. "Oh, all right. We'll pull off at the next town and grab something at a drive-through. But we can't stop for more than a couple of minutes—we have to get right back on the road."

"I can't believe we're doing this," she muttered.

Did she think *he* was enjoying it? "Well, if you hadn't given the bunny to that kid of yours, we wouldn't *be* in this predicament."

"And if you hadn't tied the ring to the bunny, he couldn't have lost it," Natty countered. "What were you thinking of, anyway, to do such a silly thing?"

Beau hunched his shoulders. "I was trying to be . . . romantic."

Natty's tone softened. "Oh, Beau, it *was* romantic. Or it would have been, if Cole hadn't interrupted." She leaned over and kissed his cheek. "What kind of ring is it?"

Well, that was better. This wasn't the time or the place for a proposal, but maybe a hint wouldn't hurt. "Oh, a diamond," he said with studied nonchalance.

"A diamond? Oh, Beau . . ." Natty's voice was breathless with anticipation and hope.

Beau smiled to himself. If he'd known it would have this effect on her, he would've told her before. Maybe now she'd understand how important this was.

A confused look replaced the adoration on her face. "But why does Mr. Peterson want it back?"

He squirmed. "I accidentally took the wrong ring."

"You mean the wrong size? Or shape?"

"No, I, uh . . . got the cubic zirconia and the diamond mixed up."

"But why would Mr. Peterson fire you for taking a CZ by mistake?"

Beau kept silent, not knowing how to explain, but Natty was too quick on the uptake.

"You mean you were going to give *me* the CZ?"

"Yes, but only until I could afford—"

She punched him in the arm. "You cheapskate. Is that all I'm worth to you?"

"No, it's just that I wanted to give you something big and splashy, something you'd really like. I figured I'd exchange it later for a real diamond."

"Just how big is this diamond, anyway?"

He swallowed hard. "Seven carats."

"Seven?" She turned suddenly quiet. "No wonder Mr. Peterson wants it back. It must be worth a fortune."

"It is, and I really can't afford to pay for its loss— or lose my job. You see now why I need it?"

"Yes, I see. But I still can't believe you're so cheap."

He cringed inwardly. "I'm not. Honest. When we find the diamond, I'll get my money back on the CZ and buy you a real diamond." Before she could misunderstand, he said, "A *smaller* one, okay?"

"All right," Natty said. "But this time I'll go with you to pick it out."

"Okay," Beau muttered. He had a feeling this little escapade was going to cost him a lot more before he was through.

MEG YAWNED AND STRETCHED in the confines of the car. They'd finally reached the outskirts of El Paso, but there was still no sign of her truck. There was no way she'd find Baby now. She sighed and spared a moment of sorrow for her rabbit...and her lost dream of living in San Antonio.

She glanced at Cole. Well, one dream was down the tubes—how about the other? Having an exciting fling with Cole might go a long way toward making that existence a little more palatable.

But...did she actually have the nerve to follow through with her seduction plans? What if he laughed at her? Worse, what if he pitied her?

Meg almost changed her mind, but images of solemn widowers with broods of children rose to haunt her. Before she resigned herself to that fate, it was definitely worth risking a moment's embarrassment to try and seduce Cole.

Okay, that was settled...but *how* was she going to do it? Various romantic scenarios flashed through her mind, but since she didn't have a slinky harem outfit, a hot tub or a Marilyn Monroe body, none of them would work. She'd just have to play it by ear and hope Cole caught on quickly enough to take the initiative.

She shifted uncomfortably in the car seat, realizing she couldn't seduce him dressed like this. She felt grungy and sticky—and that wasn't exactly conducive to romance. "Cole? We're going to need a change of clothes tomorrow. There's a discount store over there. Do you think—"

"Good idea," he said, and pulled off into the parking lot.

Once inside, they split up, Cole and Luke heading for one part of the store while Meg and Susie headed for the other, promising to meet in forty-five minutes.

Meg bought a collar for Lady, picked out some pants and blouses for the next couple of days, then headed for the underwear. She selected some pretty, lacy ones and indulged herself in daydreaming about what would happen if Cole was to see them on her.

Susie tugged on her arm then, and Meg gazed at the little girl with dawning realization. A child? Yes, that was also a distinct possibility—unless she did something about it.

What could she do to ensure she didn't get pregnant? She'd always expected that the man would take care of that, but if Cole didn't know he was going to be seduced, he might not have the right . . . accessories available.

Condoms. She needed condoms.

Her face flushed with embarrassment. Oh, no, she was going to have to buy those things, here, now. But could she do it without dying of mortification?

After thinking about it, Meg decided she could. Better the mortification than the alternative. The next question was, where were they? Near the medicines, maybe?

She hurried off to that part of the store, and when she finally found them, she checked her watch. Okay, she had ten minutes to go. If she did this quickly, she could check out before Cole did, so that he didn't see what was in her basket.

She glanced at the wall of contraceptive products. Now what? She squinted at the fine print. Lubricated . . . ribbed . . . ultrasensitive—for heaven's sake, which should she get? There were too many choices.

Just how did you go about choosing a condom for a man, anyway? She could just see herself going up to Cole and casually inquiring whether he preferred lubricated or ribbed—and just how sensitive did he want it to be, anyway? Yeah, right.

She'd just have to go it alone this time. Her hand hovered over one brand that seemed to have most of these things, but then another package caught her eye, announcing a new large size.

She gulped. What about the others? She checked them—no size listed. Now what? Would she offend him if she didn't pick up the large size? But what if she did and it was too big? Would it fall off? Oh, that would be fun.

She stood there, wasting precious time while she dithered. Oh, to heck with it. She'd just grab one and go. If he didn't like her choice, *he* could pick it out next time. Closing her eyes, she grabbed a package and shoved it under a blouse in her basket, then hurried to the next section to buy the necessary toiletries.

Once that was done, she glanced at her watch. Only one minute left. Darn. She'd just have to head up to the cash registers and hope Cole didn't watch as she paid for her purchases.

Cole and Luke were already waiting on the other side of the registers, packages in hand. Cole approached her, and Meg panicked. What was she going to do now? She'd just die if he saw the condoms in her cart.

Could she just pretend the package had fallen in by accident and remove it with a nonchalant flick of the wrist? No, she needed those condoms, or she wouldn't be able to put her seduction plans into effect.

She glanced down at Susie, and inspiration struck. "Cole, I think the kids have to go to the bathroom again. Would you mind taking them this time?"

Just as Meg expected, Susie nodded her head and Luke followed suit.

"Okay," Cole said. "Let's go."

Meg breathed a sigh of relief, then unloaded her basket as fast as she could and paid for her purchases. She just hoped she was going to be able to *use* these condoms, now that she'd gone to so much trouble to get them.

Luckily, Cole came back after she was finished, and they headed out again. Now they just needed somewhere to sleep. She turned to Cole. "There's a Howard Johnson's at the next exit. My family always stays there, so I know they allow animals in the room. Besides, I have reservations there for the day after tomorrow, and I need to cancel them."

"Sounds fine to me," Cole said, and steered the car off at the next exit.

He parked and started to get out of the car, but Meg stopped him. "No, you wait here with the kids. I'll get us a room."

"But—"

"I insist. You're being kind enough to help me find Baby, so the least I can do is pay your expenses." She glared at him, daring him to contradict her.

He must have seen the determination in her eyes, for he nodded and closed the car door. "All right, but I haven't been much help yet."

Meg got out of the car and closed the door. "You will be," she murmured with a smile. "You will be."

She paid for the room and canceled her other reservation, then gathered her traveling companions and steered them toward the room.

Cole glanced at the two queen-size beds, then at Meg with an enigmatic expression. "One room?"

Though she could feel a blush coming on, Meg forced herself to meet his gaze. "Is that okay? I can't afford two, and I figured Luke and Susie would be chaperon enough." She widened her eyes and tried to look guileless.

"Oh. Sure. No problem."

She gave him a beaming smile. "Good." Now, if only the rest of her plan would go as smoothly...

Luke yawned, right on cue.

"Looks like we need to get the little ones to bed," Meg said. "Bath time."

Susie frowned. "Do we hafta?"

"Yes, Susie, you have to. It's eight o'clock, and after playing with that dog, you're both filthy."

Luke looked up at his father with an endearing grin. "Lady sleep wif *me*."

"Oh, no, she won't. You are *not* going to become attached to that dog." The stubborn expression on Cole's face matched the one on his son's.

Luke hugged the little dog closer. "Yes," he declared.

"No," Cole insisted.

Seeing that this could soon degenerate into a no-win situation, Meg intervened. "We'll discuss that later, *after* the baths. And first up is Lady—she's not sleeping with anyone until she gets clean." She had to wash the dog first, or the children would get dirty all over again when they tried to play with her.

Lady wagged her bushy tail and barked once by way of punctuation.

"See," Meg said. "She agrees with me."

Luke giggled, and the tension in the room evaporated. Cole gave her another one of those you're-good-with-kids looks, and Meg grimaced to herself. She wanted to be Cole's lover, not Luke's nanny. But how was she going to convince Cole that her talents were better utilized in the other direction? She still wasn't sure, but she knew she had to get the others out of the way first.

She steered the dog into the bathroom and plopped her in the bathtub. Meg sighed in resignation. She seemed to be spending the entire trip in one bathroom or another, cleaning up after children and animals.

She turned the water on, and Lady yelped, scrabbling to get away. It was all Meg could do to keep the wriggling, desperate dog in the tub, and she had no idea how she was going to wet her down, let alone shampoo her. The kids were no help as they giggled and leaped around the room, encouraging the dog to make a break for it.

She heard a deep chuckle behind her, and glanced over her shoulder to see Cole lounging against the doorjamb, grinning at her.

"Yeah, yeah, very funny. Could you give me a hand here?" She made a lunging grab for the dog's back feet and grimaced when Lady's tail smacked her in the face.

Cole laughed again and came to her rescue. Kneeling next to her at the tub, he eyed the muddy dog dubiously. "Shall I wash or rinse?"

Meg chuckled. "Your job is to keep her still and in the tub while I wash her."

Somehow, between the two of them, they managed to bathe the squirming puppy, but not before every square foot of the bathroom was spattered with dirty water. When they were done, the dog was clean, but the bathroom looked like a war zone—on the losing side.

"Hold her while I get something to dry her with," Meg directed.

She grabbed a towel and wrapped it around the dog, rendering her immobile. Meg paused for a moment with the dog still in the tub, worn out by the fight.

"And I thought Luke was hard to bathe," Cole exclaimed as he straightened.

They exchanged an amused glance, and Meg's breath caught in her throat as their gazes locked. Their shared task had brought them close together, so that the side of Cole's long, lean leg was pressed up against hers. They were hip to hip, and if she leaned back and to the right just a little...

Boldly, she did so and found herself resting against Cole's strong, broad chest. Warmth flooded through her, stirring flickering feelings of excitement all through her body. She lifted her gaze to his with agonizing slowness and caught her breath when she realized their lips were only inches apart.

His gaze flicked downward, and hers followed. She saw her wet shirt plastered against her breasts, the outlines of her nipples clearly showing through the shirt. Meg gasped softly. When she went braless this morning, she hadn't expected to look like an entrant in a wet T-shirt contest. Embarrassed, she crossed her arms over her breasts.

Damn—why had she done that? She *wanted* him to look at her, didn't she? Now she'd shattered the mood.

Cole grinned and flicked the end of her nose with his finger. "You have brown splotches all over your face . . . and I don't think they're freckles."

Oh, my Lord, I must look a fright. The kids pushed in to pet the dog in the tub as Meg scrambled up from the floor to gaze at herself in the mirror.

Splotches? *Smears* was more like it—and her hair was so wet and bedraggled that she looked like something the dog had dragged in. Some seductress.

She bit back a wail of despair and considered her options. She still had time to get cleaned up and put her plan into effect after the children went to sleep. She scrubbed at her face to get the worst of the dirt off, then glanced over at Cole, who was busy rubbing Lady dry. "Why don't you rinse out the tub and start a bath for the kids? I've got some phone calls to make."

"Sure," he said agreeably.

Meg sighed and went in the other room to cancel the rest of her San Antonio reservation so she wouldn't get charged for the extra days, then called Pops to remind him to take his medicine. He was querulous again, wanting to know how she was and what she was doing, but she deflected his questions, not wanting to worry the old man or admit that she'd lost the bet— yet.

Assured he would take his medicine, she hung up as Luke and Susie bounced into the room with towels wrapped around them, their cheeks bright and rosy, flushed from their baths.

Cole leaned lazily against the doorjamb. "Next?"

Damn. Did he have any idea how sexy he looked in that pose? She tried to find something seductive and provocative to say...like an offer to share the shower with him. Unfortunately, she couldn't get the words out. "Uh...you go first. I'll just get the little ones into bed while you shower, then I'll take mine. Okay?"

He nodded. "Whatever you say."

Cole rooted through his shopping bag, then tossed Luke's pajamas to her and took the rest into the bathroom.

Meg sighed as she took Susie's nightgown out of her suitcase and cajoled the giggling children into their nightclothes. She'd just had her chance and she'd blown it. Now what was she going to do? Well, she wasn't going to give up that easily. To start with, she'd make it obvious that she and Cole would have to share a bed. She tucked both kids in one bed, somehow convincing them that clean, dry sheets did not mix well with wet puppies.

Cole emerged from the bathroom wearing nothing but a pair of gray gym shorts and a towel around his neck. Meg gulped and couldn't stop her greedy gaze from wandering over the well-developed muscles of his tanned chest, and down to his rock-hard stomach, where his shorts rode low, tantalizing her with speculations about what lay beneath.

Cole grimaced and gestured with the towel. "Sorry—I don't usually even wear this much to bed, but I figured under the circumstances..."

"Uh, sure. No problem." He normally slept in the nude? She shrugged in seeming nonchalance, wanting to tell him not to bother with clothes, but was unable to voice the words. "I'll, uh, just take my shower now." *Oh, yeah, brilliant repartee, Hollingsworth. He'll really think you're hot now.*

"Okay." Cole moved away from the doorway, but stopped short, seeing both kids in one bed, their weary eyelids already drooping. And Lady, the scamp, had jumped back up on the bed and was lying at the foot, nose tucked between her paws.

Cole raised a questioning eyebrow at Meg.

Feeling a flush creep up her neck, Meg blurted out a fib. "I— They couldn't decide who got to sleep with Lady, so this seemed a good compromise. I'll move Susie later."

Cole gave her a quizzical look, but nodded, and Meg fled to the bathroom. She closed the door behind her and leaned against it, grateful for the respite. Damn. She'd blown it again. If she wasn't careful, she'd mess everything up.

She undressed and turned the welcome water of the shower on her filthy body. She was having second thoughts, not to mention third and fourth ones. She wasn't cut out to be a seductress, and she'd undoubtedly make a fool of herself. Was it worth it?

Images flashed through her mind. Cole's devastating kiss, the warmth of his body next to hers at the tub, the way he looked in those shorts... Oh, yeah. It was worth it. Meg was tired of playing it safe. Tonight, she was going to howl.

Feeling much better, Meg dried off, then paused. What should she wear? She'd forgotten to get herself a nightgown, and she couldn't very well traipse out in the altogether. Of course, it would probably achieve the results she wanted, but it wasn't exactly... subtle.

And since she'd washed her T-shirt, she couldn't put that back on, either. She dug around in the bags, looking for her new clothes, and found Cole's button-down shirt.

Excited, she pulled it out. Just the ticket. In the movies, women were always wearing men's shirts and looking incredibly sexy. If it worked for them, maybe it could work for her.

She pulled on the shirt and a clean pair of lacy white bikini underwear, then stood on tiptoe to see herself in the mirror and drooped in disappointment. She looked like she was wearing her older brother's clothes. It wasn't exactly the effect she wanted, and with her face scrubbed clean, she looked wholesome, like the girl next door. Some makeup would help, but it was in the other room. If she went to retrieve it, Cole would get suspicious.

Well, what about her other assets? She tousled her wet hair, and her red corkscrew curls fell into place. With a little imagination, she could believe they made her look wanton. Okay, how about her expression? She pouted at the mirror. Better, but still a long way from sexy.

Maybe some cleavage? She unbuttoned another button, but the results were disappointing. Only a push-up bra would help with that problem, and she didn't have one of those, either.

Despondent, Meg sat on the tub and frowned. Hell, she just wasn't the seductive type, but she'd have to do the best with what she had. And just in case she was successful ... she grabbed the bag and took out the package of condoms. She opened it, pulled out one of the packets and stuck it in the pocket of the shirt.

Okay, it's now or never. Meg took a deep breath and opened the door. Feeling silly, she lounged against the door frame, arching her back to thrust her small breasts into prominence. Wondering if she looked as awkward as she felt, she fluffed her curls and glanced around to see what effect it had on Cole.

The children were fast asleep, and Cole was sitting on the other bed, just hanging up the phone. "I was trying to reach Natalie to let her know Luke ... is okay...."

His voice trailed off as his gaze traveled down her body and snagged on her bare legs.

"I'm sorry," Meg said. "I forgot to get something to wear at the store. I don't usually wear anything to bed, either, but as you said, considering the circumstances ..." It was a bald-faced lie, but for once, she didn't care. It was fun turning the tables to making him think of *her* nude.

She saw his swift intake of breath and smiled to herself. *Bull's-eye.*

Emboldened by the success of her strategy, she said, "You don't mind if I wear your shirt, do you? Would you rather I took it off?" She half smiled at him, her fingers poised over the top button.

"No, no. That's all right. Keep it. It looks a whole lot better on you, anyway."

Meg murmured her thanks and suppressed a grin. This was fun. Maybe she had enough equipment after all. She walked into the room, more confident now, and trailed her hand across the dresser. Leaning over, she peered out the window blinds, letting the shirt ride up so he could get a view of her lacy panties.

She glanced out the corner of her eye to see that he was indeed taking advantage of the view. Elated with the progress of her seduction so far, Meg straightened and turned, languorously stretching as she moved toward him. Keeping her voice low and throaty, she asked, "So, is it time for bed yet?"

Cole gave her a wary glance and stood, backing away slightly. "What game are you playing here, Meg?"

Meg moved closer and placed her palms against his furred chest. His muscles tightened beneath her caressing hands, and she reveled in the feeling of power it gave her. "Game? I'll let you guess." She licked her lips and smiled. "But here's a hint—it's a full-contact sport."

Cole gave her a slow smile and ran his hands down over her shoulders and across her back, pulling her tight against him. Her senses swam with the force of his sheer male presence.

She exulted when he bent to taste her lips, but instead of the sweet kiss she'd expected, he crushed her lips beneath his with an intense hunger.

A delicious shudder heated her body as she responded with equal fervor. *This* was what she'd been waiting for. "Yes," she breathed on a lingering sigh when Cole pulled back.

He gazed at her searchingly, and his voice was husky as he asked, "What exactly are the rules of this game?"

Heady with the sensations he aroused in her, Meg felt free for the first time in her life—free to let go, to become the impulsive free spirit she'd always wanted to be. "No rules." She trailed a hand down his back and flashed him a wicked grin. "We just keep on playing until somebody scores."

Cole chuckled, then bent to lift her effortlessly in his arms. Keeping his smoldering gaze firmly on hers, he deposited her with infinite gentleness on the bed, then bowed his head to feather kisses down her neck, toward the hollow between her breasts.

Taut with anticipation, Meg held her breath as he reached for the top button of her shirt.

"Daddy?" came a small voice.

Cole stiffened, and Meg peered over his shoulder to see Luke patting his father on the back.

"Sleep wif you?" Luke asked. "Me scared."

Meg froze for a moment, then clambered from the bed. How could she have forgotten the children?

Cole's glance was apologetic. "Sure, sport, climb in."

He rearranged the bedclothes so Luke could join him under them. Unsure what to do, Meg just stood there. "Now what?" she whispered.

Cole gave her a rueful half grin. "Well, I don't think this was designed to be a spectator sport. We might as well throw in the towel."

Meg grimaced and conceded defeat. He was right. She couldn't imagine making love under the curious gaze of his son, for heaven's sake. She glanced at the bed wistfully. Making love was out of the question, but maybe she could just lie next to Cole...

His mouth softened into a tender smile. "You scared, too? Want to sleep with me?"

Meg nodded. Yes, she was scared. Scared of the mixed feelings she had for this sexy, sensitive man.

Cole patted the bed next to him. "Well, come join us, then. We'll call this game on account of... interference, and reschedule it for another time."

Meg sighed in pleasure. So there *was* going to be another time. Smiling, she crawled into bed with him and sighed as Cole wrapped his arms around her and settled her against him, spoon-fashion.

"But no squirming," Cole growled, "or I won't be responsible for the consequences."

Meg smiled to herself. So he *did* find her desirable. For now, that was enough. She settled into his embrace, overly conscious of the strong male who cuddled her in his arms—and of the small one on the other side of him. Somehow she refrained from moving, and fell asleep fantasizing about what would have happened had it just been the two of them.

She woke to find herself surrounded by a cocoon of warmth. Blinking sleepily, she snuggled into the warm bodies around her and sighed. Loving tenderness enveloped her, comforted her.

Meg tried to urge her brain into gear. Where was she, and why did she feel so wonderful? She took stock of her surroundings. Sometime during the night, they had all migrated to one bed.

She was lying on her side, her head pillowed comfortably on Cole's shoulder, her arm across his chest. Susie was snuggled up to Meg's other side, and Luke lay curled in his father's opposite arm. Even Lady snoozed in the open space between Meg's calves. She closed her eyes and sighed. How cozy—just like a family.

Family? Meg's eyes flew open, and she scrambled out of bed, not caring who she woke. Damn it, this warm cozy feeling was what she'd been trying to avoid in the first place. She wanted excitement, adventure—not to be sucked into a ready-made family before she had any fun.

The children stirred, and Cole stretched. His gaze turned puzzled when he glanced at her face. "What's wrong?"

"Nothing."

He rose from the bed to look down at her. "Nothing? Are you sure you're not regretting what happened last night?"

Meg flushed, her eyes softening as she gazed into Cole's concerned eyes. "Oh, no. Never."

He grinned and leaned down to give her a tender good-morning kiss. "Good. I'd hoped for a rematch," he murmured, his breath warm against her face.

Meg's heart leaped in her chest. She did, too, but she couldn't pretend any longer. She gave him a wry smile. "Unfortunately, the sporting season is over."

"Over?"

"Yes, over." Dropping the byplay, Meg sighed. "We didn't find my truck, and I'm smart enough to realize that the odds of finding it now are very slim. I've lost Baby... and the bet."

Cole gathered her into his arms. "I'm sorry, Meg. I know how much it meant to you. What'll you do now?"

She shrugged, defeated. "Go home. It's the only thing I *can* do." How true—she was an utter failure. She'd lost her truck, her rabbit, the bet, and any chance at really living.

The only thing she *hadn't* lost was her virginity, drat the luck.

BEAU PACED the hotel room, cudgeling his brain. Mr. Peterson wanted that ring today, or Beau would lose his job. What was he going to do now?

Natty hung up the phone. "I have good news."

"What?" Beau muttered distractedly.

"Cole left a message on my voice mail—he's staying here in El Paso, too."

Beau gave her a bitter smile. "Gee, that helps. Do you have any idea how many hotels there are in a town this size, Natty? It'd take us at least two days to search them all. They're bound to slip through our fingers."

She waved a slip of paper at him. "Not when Cole left me the name and phone number of the hotel."

Chapter Six

Cole held Meg at arm's length, not believing he'd heard her correctly. "You want to quit?"

"No, I don't *want* to, but let's be realistic. Have we even glimpsed my truck? It could be anywhere in El Paso...anywhere in Texas, for that matter. There's no way we're going to find it." Her shoulders slumped, and defeat took the place of her normal jaunty attitude. "I might as well go home."

Cole hated seeing her this way. Though he'd known Meg for less than twenty-four hours, he felt he understood her better than most people he'd known all his life. This wasn't the Meg he knew.

Had *he* caused this reversal? He tipped Meg's chin up so that her gaze met his. "Are you sure this is what you want?"

She grimaced. "No, it's not what I want, but it's the only thing that makes sense. There's no use in wasting any more of your time on a wild-goose chase."

"If it's me you're worrying about, don't. I'm enjoying it." He quirked a smile at her and stroked her cheek with one hand. "Especially after last night."

Last night...her innocent seduction had been more alluring and provocative than the most practiced streetwalker's. So much so that he'd almost lost control, even though her inexperience had been obvious. He'd thought only about touching her, stroking her, needing her.

Some of his thoughts must have shown on his face, for Meg blushed and her gaze slid away from his. Cole felt a wave of tenderness wash over him.

Thank heaven for the children. If it hadn't been for them, he would've taken advantage of her invitation last night, and she'd really have something to be embarrassed about.

He opened his mouth to apologize, then thought better of it. What would he apologize for? Taking advantage of her invitation... or not taking advantage of it? Apologizing for the wrong thing was almost as bad as doing the wrong thing. He kept his mouth shut.

Meg looked up at him shyly, and he suddenly realized she was still wearing his shirt and those pristine white panties that had so aroused him last night. Unfortunately, they had the same effect on him now, and the gym shorts he wore concealed little.

He turned his back on her and pretended to check on the children. "Okay, why don't we get dressed and have some breakfast? We'll decide what to do after that."

Behind him, Meg sighed as she went into the bathroom to change clothes. Cole busied himself with waking the children and getting them dressed, and then he and the children took their turns in the bathroom when Meg was through.

When he came out, Meg had just returned from walking the dog and was feeding her. It took a little persuasion, but Luke and Susie finally understood that Lady couldn't eat breakfast with them. Knowing that puppies liked to chew on anything within reach, they closed her up in the bathroom so she couldn't do too much damage and headed for the restaurant.

While Luke and Susie chattered away about nonsensical things over breakfast, Cole studied Meg. She seemed reserved this morning, as if she were holding back. She showed little interest in the children—or in anything else, for that matter. She'd lost her animation, her sparkle.

How could he get it back? The only way he knew of was to find her rabbit for her. He wished he could roll up his sleeves and pull it out of a hat, but he was no magician.

"You know," he said, "we could call the El Paso Police Department and ask them to keep an eye out for your truck."

"Sure. Fine. Whatever. It doesn't really matter."

How could she say that, when all her dreams were riding on that rabbit? Taken aback, Cole said, "That's their job, Meg. They're good at it. At least try it."

She shrugged. "Even if they find the truck, there's no guarantee Baby will still be in it—or what shape he'll be in."

"True, but how do you know until you try? What about your dream of living in San Antonio?"

She shook her head. "The dream's dead. How long do you think it would take them to find my truck? Two days? Three? A week? By then, the fair will be over and I'll have lost my last chance of winning the bet." Her shoulders drooped as she toyed with her food.

He wouldn't admit it to her, but he was glad. This way, she wouldn't get sucked into the big city—and he'd be able to see more of her when he moved to Lingston. But that was small comfort when he saw how badly she was taking it.

Luke must have sensed a change in Meg, too, for he was staring earnestly at her, his small brow furrowed in concern. "Aunt Meg, watch me," he said, then stuck a large forkful of pancake in his mouth. When that only elicited a wan smile from her, he wiggled his eyebrows, then giggled, watching her with merriment in his eyes.

Meg's smile grew a little wider, but it didn't reach her eyes. Luke swallowed his food, but didn't give up. He glanced around the restaurant, then pointed out the window in excitement. "Look, Aunt Meg, a wed twuck."

Meg glanced out the window, then did a double take. A look of shock spread over her face. "Oh, my Lord, I don't believe it," she muttered.

"What?"

She pointed out at the parking lot. "My truck. That's my truck."

Cole whirled around to stare in disbelief. The odds against the thief's choosing the same hotel were astronomical—especially when the truck was parked only a couple of spaces from their room. "Are you sure?"

"No, not totally—I can't see the license number from here. But there's one way to find out." She rose to head out the door.

He held out a restraining hand. "Whoa, wait a minute." He knew he wouldn't be able to stop her, but he could at least help. "I'm going with you." He tossed a couple of bills on the table and headed out the door after her, herding the kids behind.

As they neared the truck, she narrowed her gaze. "That's it—that's my license number." All of a sudden, her body positively vibrated with excitement—her animation and sparkle were back.

She increased her pace, but Cole grabbed her arm to stop her. "Wait. The thief might still be around."

"But I have to check on Baby."

"Not with the kids around."

Meg glanced down at them and chewed her lip. "Oh, yeah. I forgot. Well, you take them to the room, and I'll check out the truck."

No way was Cole going to let Meg investigate that truck without him. He wasn't crazy about leaving the kids alone, even for a few minutes, but he wanted even less to expose them to danger.

Then again, the truck was only a few yards away from the room, and they'd only be gone a couple of minutes. He'd have to leave them alone—it was his only option.

"No, I'm coming with you. The kids will be all right in the room for a little while. And that's all it's going to be—right?"

Meg agreed, and they went to the room, let the dog out of the bathroom, then turned the television on to keep the kids occupied. After threatening them with a fate worse than death if they so much as moved a muscle, Cole paused on his way out the door with his hand on the knob. "Why don't you let me do this, and you stay here?"

She shook her head. "You won't be able to tell if Baby's all right or not. He's my rabbit, and I'm going to take care of him."

Cole sighed. It looked like he was going to lose this round, too.

Meg pushed at him. "C'mon, I need to see how Baby's doing."

Cole cracked the door open and peered out. He didn't see anyone around, so he opened the door the rest of the way. Meg pushed past him and hurried over to the truck. He followed more leisurely, checking out the nearby cars and the surroundings.

She leaned over and looked in the back of the truck, then slammed her hand against the side. "Damn. Baby's gone. They even took his cage." She chewed her lip, looking distressed. "I wonder what they did with him?"

She glanced around inside as if looking for a clue. "Hey, what's this?" She reached down inside the truck bed for something Cole couldn't see.

"C'mon," he urged. "Let's go." The longer they stayed here, the more chance there was that the thief would show up. He didn't want Meg around when that happened.

"Just a second. It's caught on something."

Once she tugged it free, Cole grabbed her arm and dragged her away from the truck, back to the relative safety of the room.

They closed the door behind them, and Luke and Susie looked up at them with guilty expressions. No wonder. It had only been a couple of minutes, but that had been long enough for Lady to find a box of tissues and reduce them to shredded bits of white fluff strewn all over the room.

Lady looked up from where she was gnawing on the empty box and barked once, wagging her tail. Cole couldn't help but grin. The silly dog looked so proud of herself, he didn't have the heart to chastise her. He'd let Meg take care of disciplining the puppy. After all, Lady was supposed to be *her* dog.

Luke grinned in relief when he saw Cole's smile, then glanced at what Meg was carrying. "Puppy!"

"No, sweetie," Meg said as she glanced at the bedraggled stuffed animal in her hand. "It's not a puppy, it's a bunny." She looked thunderstruck and turned to Cole at the same time the thought occurred to him. "A bunny? This must be what Beau was looking for."

Cole turned to Luke. "Did Mommy give you this?"

Luke reached out his arms. "Mine."

"Well, that clears up one mystery. I remember Natalie handed Luke a stuffed animal in San Antonio and told him it was a puppy. He must have dropped it in the back of the truck just before you came running out."

"Mine," Luke repeated.

Meg gave Cole a hesitant look. "Should I? It was protected by the feed box, so it's not very dirty."

Cole shrugged. "I don't see anything special about it. Nothing that would make Beau want it so badly anyway. Why not let Luke play with it?"

Meg handed Luke the toy and turned a resolute face to Cole. "Now what?"

"Well, you still have your keys, so I suppose you could just take your truck back . . . but I wouldn't recommend it."

Meg shook her head. "No. I want to get the man who stole my truck and find out what he did with Baby. Can't we just wait for him to show up so you can arrest him?"

"Sorry, no can do. I'm way out of my jurisdiction. But let's call the El Paso police and have them make the arrest. I assume you can prove the truck is yours?"

"Yes—if he's left the registration in the glove compartment." She shrugged. "If I have to, I can have Pops go to town and fax me a copy of my title."

She hesitated. "But what if the thief comes before they get here? Shouldn't we watch for him so we can make a citizen's arrest or something?"

Just what he needed—a thrill-seeking civilian trying to take down a felon. "Okay, you call the police and wait for their arrival. I'll watch the truck from outside."

"But won't a police car scare him off?"

Cole shrugged. "Maybe, but that's better than confronting him, isn't it?"

She didn't look convinced. "But if we don't catch him, we may never know where Baby is."

That rabbit again. "All right. Then call and explain the situation to the police, and let *them* worry about how to handle it. They're the experts."

Meg looked stubborn. "I don't want to miss anything."

"Look, if nothing else, we have to keep the kids out of harm's way. I'm trained for this—you're not. Why don't you just call the cops, then watch from the window? You can see the truck from there."

"All right," she said in an ungracious tone. "But I want to hear every detail, all right?"

Shaking his head at her quest for excitement, Cole shooed her off toward the phone and went outside to sit in the car, where he could keep an eye on the truck—and the hotel room. He was accustomed to long, boring stakeouts, but Meg wasn't. Though he doubted she'd abandon the kids, he wanted to make sure she didn't try anything foolish.

Luckily, he didn't have to wait long for something to happen. After about twenty minutes, a man walked toward the truck, whistling. He was about five foot eight, a hundred and eighty pounds, with reddish-brown hair and an open, guileless expression on his face. He didn't look much like a thief, but Cole knew better than to judge people on appearance alone.

Cole eased out of the car and strolled toward the truck. If the man passed it by, then Cole would, too, but he had a feeling . . .

Bingo. The man opened the truck door and climbed in.

Several thoughts fought for prominence in Cole's mind as he raced toward the truck. First, he'd left his

gun in San Antonio, so what the hell was he going to
do if the man had a weapon? Second, he caught a
flash of Meg's stunned face at the window and hoped
she had enough sense to stay inside. Third, he was really getting too old for this kind of crap.

He reached the truck and jerked the door open. A
look of astonishment flashed across the thief's face.
Cole grabbed a fistful of the man's shirt and tried to
yank him out of the truck, but came up short—the
man was held fast by the lap belt.

Damn. What kind of crook fastened his seat belt,
for heaven's sake? As the man dangled head down out
of the cab, his arms flailing for something to hold on
to, Cole jabbed the belt's release button and the metal
piece snapped up to smack the man in the nose.

"Yow!" He grabbed his face with both hands, losing his balance in the process.

Using the man's forward momentum, Cole half
pulled, half shoved him facedown onto the pavement
and sat on him, jerking his arm up between his shoulder blades.

Sensing a great deal of movement around him, Cole
glanced up, his body still pumping with adrenaline.
Meg ran out of the room, slamming the door behind
her, and two cars screeched to a halt next to them.

"Let him *go*," Meg cried.

"What?"

Two uniformed policeman jumped out of one car
with their guns drawn. The older one yelled,
"Freeze!"

The other car's doors opened, and Beau lurched
out. "Where's my bunny?"

Natalie took one look at the scene, and her face turned white. She scrambled out of the car, shrieking, "Where's my son?"

The cop and his partner, obviously a rookie, looked totally perplexed. Cole knew how they felt—as if they'd somehow wandered into a Keystone Cops movie by mistake.

The policemen just pointed their guns at everyone in sight as the older one bellowed, "Nobody move!"

Everyone froze, and the guns wavered from one person to the next as the policemen tried to figure out who was the most likely menace.

"Now," the older one said, gesturing with his gun at Cole. "Let him up, slowly."

Realizing the man beneath him couldn't get away very easily with two weapons trained on him, Cole did as directed, and the man clambered to his feet, holding his nose and glaring at Cole.

"You two," the cop said, gesturing at Beau and Natalie. "Stand over by them. You, too, ma'am," he said, gesturing at Meg.

The three went to stand by Cole as directed, and he just concentrated on catching his breath and keeping an eye on the thief, in case he decided to make a break for it.

"Now," the cop said, "which of you is Ms. Hollingsworth?"

Meg raised her hand. "Me," she said in a tentative voice.

"Could you show us some identification?" he asked.

"I don't have any with me...it's in the hotel room."

The older of the two cops waved his pistol at her. "Okay. Johnson, you go with her to get it. The rest of you stay here."

The rookie, Johnson, escorted Meg to the room, and Cole squinted at the older cop's name tag. "Sergeant Hernandez?"

"What?"

"I'm Detective McKenzie, with the San Antonio Police Department. If you'll allow me..." He gestured toward the shield in his back pocket.

Hernandez frowned. "All right, but take it out slowly and toss it over here."

Cole did so, and Hernandez picked up the leather case. "McKenzie, huh?" He relaxed and tossed it back. "What's the deal here?"

Cole nodded toward the red-haired man. "This is the man you want. I caught him stealing Ms. Hollingsworth's truck. The other two are harmless."

Meg and Johnson returned, and babble broke out again.

"I did not—"

"I'll give you harmless—"

"Where's Luke?"

"...my brother."

Cole looked at Meg in astonishment. "What did you say?"

"That's no thief. That's my brother, Jerry."

Jerry took his hand away from his face, and Cole could see the resemblance, now that he had it pointed out to him. "Your brother? What's he doing with your stolen truck?"

Meg turned to face Jerry, her expression stony. "That's what I'd like to know. And where's my rabbit?"

Beau screeched, "It's not your rabbit! It's *mine*."

Cole shook his head. The disheveled, tuxedo-clad man was rapidly losing any composure he might have had.

"No," Meg said. "Baby is mine. The bunny is yours."

Natalie glanced around with a frantic expression. "Where's *my* baby?"

The cops looked totally confused now, but since it was obvious that no one was going to turn violent any time soon, with the possible exception of Beau, they holstered their weapons. Hernandez turned to Cole. "McKenzie, do you think you could explain what's going on here? I'll have to file a report...."

"*I'll* tell you what happened—" Beau began.

"No," Hernandez said. "I asked Detective McKenzie to explain this mess."

Cole shook his head. "I'll try. Why don't we all go into the hotel room and sort this out?"

"Good idea," Hernandez said.

"No," Beau said. "I want my bunny *now*."

Hernandez looked at Beau as if he were deranged. "Not now. You'll get your property *after* we sort this all out."

"But my bunny—"

"That's enough!" Hernandez roared. "One more peep out of you, buddy, and I'll make sure you never see your bunny again."

Cole couldn't help it—he grinned.

Hernandez shook his head and rolled his eyes heavenward. "I can't believe I just said that."

It was too much. Cole doubled over and howled with laughter. Meg, Jerry and the two cops joined him, but Beau and Natalie seemed to find it decidedly unfunny.

As Cole wiped tears of laughter from his eyes, he reflected that that was what had been wrong with his marriage—Natalie had no sense of humor. Meg, on the other hand, was chuckling right along with him, though she was the one most wronged in this whole situation.

Beau opened his mouth to say something, but glanced at Hernandez's expression and clamped it shut.

"Johnson," Hernandez instructed. "If that man opens his mouth one more time, gag him."

"You got it," Johnson said, and looked at Beau with a hopeful expression.

Beau just glared, turned up his nose and sniffed in disdain.

Hernandez gestured, waving them into the room. Everyone trooped in.

Luke glanced up from the TV and smiled. "Hi, Mommy."

"My baby!" Natalie ran over to squeeze the astounded Luke. "Oh, why were you stolen away from me?"

Cole frowned. Had Natalie been taking acting classes again? It sure sounded like it, but she needed a lot more practice, if this was the result.

"Kidnapped?" Hernandez turned a beady eye on Beau.

Beau looked offended and shook his head vehemently, but kept his mouth shut.

"No," Natalie cried. "Not him. *Him,*" she declared, pointing at Cole.

"Don't be ridiculous," Cole said. "Why would I kidnap my own son? Especially when I have custody of him?" Natalie was obviously distraught. Then again, it was understandable. Being in Beau's company for two days could do that to a person.

Meg chimed in. "That's right. Besides, Luke sneaked into the car when no one was looking to get away from Beau, didn't you, Luke?"

With all eyes on him, Luke turned shy, but nodded.

Hernandez looked as though he'd believe anything of Beau. "Okay, everyone sit down, and let's figure this out."

Natalie clutched Luke to her suddenly maternal bosom, and appropriated one of the two chairs in the room. Beau took the other, and the rest of them seated themselves on the beds, with the exception of Hernandez and Johnson, who stood watching all of them, especially Beau.

Cole glanced around. The puppy was nowhere in sight. Meg must have locked her up in the bathroom again—after she cleaned up the mess.

Hernandez glared at the television, and Meg turned it off.

"Now," Hernandez said. "McKenzie, start from the beginning."

"Well, I had arranged to meet Natalie." He nodded at her to indicate who he was talking about.

"Your wife?"

"*Ex*-wife," they said in unison.

The cop's eyebrows rose, but he nodded.

"Anyway, I dropped Luke off so he could spend the weekend with her, and then Meg—Ms. Hollingsworth—came running out screaming that someone had stolen her truck and her baby."

Meg intervened. "Not my baby—"

"I know, I know. But I thought that's what she said. He actually stole her rabbit."

Beau made a choking sound, and everyone turned to look at him, but he remained silent.

"So," Hernandez said, "how did you get a rabbit mixed up with a baby?"

"The baby's name is Rabbit," Cole explained, then shook his head, feeling his ears turn warm. "I mean . . . the rabbit's name is Baby. You see?"

"I think so," the cop said doubtfully. "Then the bunny . . . rabbit . . . is actually hers?"

"The rabbit is, but the bunny isn't."

Hernandez looked puzzled. "Would you mind running that by me again?"

"Sorry, I have to back up. When I dropped Luke off, Beau gave Natalie a stuffed animal, which she handed to Luke, my son."

"Beau?" Hernandez asked.

Cole indicated Beau with a nod of his head, and Hernandez muttered, "It figures." Louder, he said, "So the boy had the bunny?"

"No, puppy!" cried Luke.

"Puppy?" Hernandez seemed to have lost the thread of the conversation.

"Yes, Luke had the bunny, but he thought it was a puppy." Seeing the confused look on the cop's face, Cole said, "Never mind, that's not important. What is important is that Luke apparently dropped the bunny in the back of Meg's truck just before it was stolen, and Beau has been trying to get it back ever since."

Hernandez looked relieved at finally finding something he could understand. "So Beau stole the truck to get the bunny back?"

"No, Jerry stole the truck," Cole said, and pointed at the man, who had been very quiet up to now.

"Ms. Hollingsworth's brother?"

"Yes."

"Why would her brother steal her truck?"

"I don't know," Cole said, "but I bet it has something to do with the missing rabbit."

"*Which* missing rabbit?" Hernandez asked in exasperation.

"Baby," Cole and Meg said in unison.

"A baby rabbit?" Hernandez said in a faint voice.

Cole opened his mouth to explain again, but the older cop just waved his hand and sighed. "Never mind. I don't want to know. Tell me about the truck."

"Yes," Meg said, turning a steely eye on Jerry. "Tell us about the truck. Why did you take it—and what have you done with Baby?"

Jerry's face flamed red, and he looked as though he'd like to crawl under the covers and hide.

"Come on," Hernandez barked, obviously glad to find *someone* who appeared to have committed a crime. "Answer your sister."

Jerry gulped and muttered something unintelligible.

"What? Speak up, man."

"The bet," Jerry said, barely choking out the words.

"The bet?" Meg screeched, and leaped to her feet. "You *creep!* You stole Baby to make me lose the bet? How could you?"

Jerry shrugged. "Pops . . ."

Meg wasn't mollified. "Why, that old coot. You mean he never meant to give the bet a fair chance?"

"He never thought you'd win—"

"And when it looked like I was going to, he decided to cheat instead? How could he do that to me?" Meg advanced on her brother and slugged him. "How could *you?*"

Jerry looked as if he thought *he* was the victim.

"Answer her," Cole said in a harsh voice.

"I'll do what I damn well *want.*"

Meg slugged him again. "What about me? Did you ever think about what *I* want?"

Jerry looked extremely puzzled. "But you never complained. We thought it was just a phase you were going through."

Meg stiffened, and managed to control her temper. "A phase?" she repeated. She deflated, as if all the hope had been knocked out of her. "You thought it was a phase? Obviously, you've never known me."

Exactly what Cole had just been thinking. How could Jerry and her grandfather have treated her this way, as if she were of no consequence? Couldn't they see the warm, vibrant woman screaming to get away from the restricted life they led?

Obviously not, from the puzzled look on Jerry's face.

"Never mind," Meg said in a resigned tone. "Just tell me what you've done with Baby."

Jerry wriggled in discomfort. "I . . . sold him."

"You *sold* my rabbit? To who?"

Meg raised her clenched fist again, and Jerry cringed but said, "To a breeder."

When Meg just closed her eyes in frustrated rage, Hernandez intervened. "Would you like to press charges?"

"I ought to," Meg declared, but her expression softened when she looked at her brother's face. "But no. At least not if he gives me the name and address of the breeder he sold him to—and agrees to make Pops abide by the original terms of the bet."

"Bet?" the rookie asked.

Hernandez gave him a stern look. "Don't ask. I don't think I could stand any more explanations." He turned to Jerry. "Do you agree to her terms?"

Jerry nodded.

"All right, then you're free to go."

Beau stood, waving his arms, his face purpling with the effort it took to keep his mouth shut.

Hernandez sighed. "All right, what do you have to say?"

"Don't let him get away until I find my bunny!"

"Back to that again, are we?" He gave a resigned look around the room. "Would anyone care to explain it to me this time?" He speared Beau with a glance. "Not you." He turned to give Cole an equally malevolent glare. "Not you, either. Last time you tried to explain it, I got a headache. Ms. Hollingsworth?"

Meg nodded. "It's very simple, really. Luke dropped the stuffed rabbit—the bunny—in the back of my truck, with the real rabbit, named Baby. When Jerry took my truck, he then had both the rabbit and the bunny in the back, and Beau and Cole started chasing after the rabbits." She paused. "Are you still with me?"

Hernandez nodded, so Meg continued. "When we stopped in San Antonio to talk to a very nice policeman, Luke sneaked from Beau's car to Cole's. Naturally, we were a little confused when Beau said he was looking for a bunny, because we thought he meant my rabbit. You see?"

Hernandez sighed, and a smile spread across his face for the first time since they'd met him. "Yes, I do see." He turned to Cole. "Why couldn't you have just said that?"

Cole shrugged. He thought that was what he *had* said.

Beau looked as though he were at the end of his patience. "You forgot the most important part—where's the bunny *now?*"

"Here," Meg said. "In our room."

"*Our* room?" Jerry repeated with raised eyebrows. "What do you mean, *our* room? Have you been shar-

ing a room with this guy?'' He glared at Cole as if he
were the devil incarnate.

Hell of a time for Jerry to finally start acting like a
brother. Not knowing how Meg wanted to handle this,
Cole turned to her for his cue as Natalie stared in
openmouthed astonishment.

Meg turned bright red. ''Yes, but it's not what you
think.''

''You spent the night with him in a hotel room, and
it's not what I think? Oh, sure.'' Jerry sneered, appearing happy he'd finally regained the upper hand.

Jerry's suspicions weren't entirely unfounded, but
it was difficult to stomach his attitude. Cole rose.
''You heard your sister. Nothing happened. Got it?''

''Yeah, right. You two were—''

''So where's the *bunny?*'' Beau yelled, interrupt-
ing.

Meg answered him. ''It's—'' She stopped herself
and gave him a puzzled look. ''Wait. What's so important about this bunny, anyway?''

''None of your *damn business,*'' Beau screamed.

The whole room seemed to rear in shock at Beau's
rudeness. Little Susie recovered first. Yelling, ''Leave
Aunt Meg *alone,*'' she ran over and kicked Beau in the
shin.

Chapter Seven

Meg stifled a grin. That was exactly what she'd wanted to do but hadn't dared.

Cole wasn't amused. He glared at Beau and growled, "Answer the lady."

"Answer... what...?" The expression on Beau's face was almost comical as he nursed his sore leg. He obviously wanted to comply, but didn't have a clue what Cole was talking about.

"What's so important about that bunny?"

Beau's gaze darted over to where Natalie was comforting Luke. He didn't get any help from that quarter. Natalie glared at him as though he were some form of fungus.

He spread his hands. "There's something attached to the ribbon around its neck."

"What's attached?"

Beau looked uneasy. "I'd, uh, rather not say."

At that, the two cops raised their eyebrows. Hernandez hooked his thumbs in his belt loops and speared Beau with a single glance. "Oh? Why not?"

Beau's eyes darted back and forth. "It's rather valuable...."

"Stolen property?"

"No, no. Well, not really."

A gleam appeared in Hernandez's eyes, and he took a step toward Beau, followed closely by Johnson. Panic flitted across Beau's face when he saw the purposeful grin on Johnson's.

Natalie pushed over to stand between them. "Oh, for heaven's sake, it's perfectly simple. Beau tied a diamond ring to the bunny." She went on to explain the circumstances and the misunderstanding.

Hernandez nodded, appearing disappointed. "So, where is it now?"

Cole shrugged. "Meg found the bunny in the truck when she was looking for Baby. She gave it to Luke, who probably gave it to Lady."

"Lady? What lady?"

"The puppy," Cole explained patiently.

Hernandez frowned. "Don't start *that* again."

Meg jumped into the fray. "The dog is in the bathroom. I think she has the bunny. Let's look, shall we?"

Beau's face lit up. He rushed to the bathroom door and jerked it open. Taking one glance at the floor, he wailed, "Noooooo..."

Had something happened to the dog? Meg darted over to peer into the room, then sighed in relief. Lady appeared to be all right, but the bunny was a goner.

The poor thing lay broken and limp under one puppy paw. Its head was ripped open, and its dismembered features mingled with shredded fur and white stuffing to lie scattered all over the bathroom. As the crowning indignity, a small pink ribbon fragment bobbled from the dog's mouth like a forked tongue.

Beau tried to snatch the ribbon to safety, but it was too late. Lady swallowed, then lolled her tongue out at them and wagged her tail.

Beau grabbed Lady by the scruff of the neck, his expression murderous. Terrified that she was about to witness a summary execution, Meg cast Cole a desperate look.

He glared at Beau. "Drop. The. Dog."

His tone was menacing enough to scare the hell out of her. What must it be doing to Beau?

Beau carefully set Lady down and turned to face Cole, his expression now desperate. "If I don't get that ring back, I'll lose my job. It was on that ribbon the dog just ate. What do *you* suggest?"

"How large is this ring?"

"Seven carats."

Cole whistled in appreciation. "Then we'd better take the dog to the vet for an X ray."

Beau smirked. "I thought you'd see it my way."

"I'm concerned about the damage it'll do to the *dog.*"

"Oh. Yes. Of course." Apparently, sincerity was *not* Beau's strong suit. "Uh, shall we go?"

Hernandez stepped forward. "Before you go, Ms. Hollingsworth, are you sure you don't want to press charges?"

"I'm sure."

"We'll leave, then." Hernandez cast a dubious glance at Beau, then looked back at Meg. "Unless you think you'll need us?"

She shook her head. "No, that's okay. I think Cole can keep him in line."

Once the cops were out the door, Beau repeated, "Shall we go?"

Meg grimaced. "I don't think we all need to take one small puppy to the vet. I'll go—she's my dog."

"You're not going without me," Beau declared. "It's my ring."

Cole raised one sardonic eyebrow. "Then I'll go along. And Jerry'd better come, too—just to make sure he doesn't take off with the truck again."

Jerry and Beau frowned, but didn't say anything.

"That's almost everyone," Meg protested.

They all turned to look at Natalie, who grimaced. "I have no desire to go." Her tone and manner expressed total disinterest in what happened to the ring—or to Beau. "I'll just stay here and watch the children."

"Good," Meg said. "Now let's find a vet who'll give us an appointment on short notice."

They found one in the telephone book who was close by and willing to see them. The four of them piled into the car with the dog, and Cole drove in total silence to the animal hospital.

Meg was glad of the silence—she had no desire to talk to any of them, especially Cole. He was trying to take over her life, too, just like Pops and Jerry. She shook her head. Men. Nothing but problems. Or as Gram would've said, "You can't live with them, and you can't live without them."

Well, Meg was certainly willing to try living without the men in her life for a while. Disappointment and pain flickered through her. How could Pops and Jerry have done this to her? Didn't they care? All of a sudden, she desperately wished her grandmother was still alive. Gram would've kicked them out and left them to fend for themselves.

That wasn't a bad idea. In fact, after she got Baby back, won the bet fair and square and moved to San Antonio, she might just become more like Gram. Jerry was Meg's *older* brother, for heaven's sake. It was time he took some responsibility for taking care of Pops. And it was time Meg started looking out for number one for a change.

Her shoulders sagged. Yeah, right. Who was she kidding? They'd never change, and she'd never be able to trust them to take care of themselves.

To heck with that. She just wanted to dump these impossible men, find Baby and continue on to the Arizona State Fair—after she got a couple of things cleared up first. She turned around to glance at her brother.

"Jerry, how long have you been planning this?"

He shrugged. "Since the last time Baby won a title."

She couldn't believe it. That had been over two months ago. "You mean you've been plotting against me all this time?"

Jerry had the grace to look guilty. "C'mon, sis. You don't really mean to hold us to the bet, do you? I thought you liked the farm."

He was so dense sometimes. Did she have to spell it out for him? "Like it? Why would I spend all that time alone in my room, reading of far-off places, of people doing different, exciting things, if I wanted to stay on the farm?''

"I just thought you liked to read."

Meg sighed. It figured. Jerry never read anything more absorbing than auto service manuals. "I do like to read," she explained. "But that's because books take me to different worlds, where life is a whole lot more interesting than living on a rabbit farm."

"Oh." Jerry didn't seem any more enlightened, but Meg decided not to explain it to him. He found it hard to understand anything beyond farming or racing cars.

She changed the subject. "Why didn't you just take Baby instead of the whole truck?" The how was easy enough to understand—he had a set of her keys.

Jerry still wouldn't meet her gaze. "We didn't want you getting suspicious, and we thought you might be if I took only the rabbit and not the truck."

"So you abandoned me in San Antonio?" How could he be so callous?

"We figured you'd call Pops right away, and he'd come get you. Why *didn't* you call him?" Jerry seemed mighty put out that she hadn't done exactly as they'd planned. That also explained why Pops had been so peevish on the phone.

"Well, Cole was there, and since he's a cop, I figured he could help me catch the thief."

"I didn't know you knew any cops in San Antonio."

"I didn't until yesterday—when you stole my truck." Good grief, had it only been yesterday? It felt like a lifetime ago. "He happened to be standing there when you drove off, and he offered to help me."

Jerry shot a dirty look at Cole, as if to say it was all Cole's fault that things hadn't turned out the way he expected. "Wait a minute. You mean you just went off with a total stranger? Meg, that's not like you. Why would you do such a thing?"

Cole saved Meg from answering. "Why do you think? Because her family stole her truck, her rabbit and her dreams, then left her to fend for herself in a strange city. Who else did she have to turn to but strangers?"

There was a slight logic problem there, but Meg didn't care. She was just glad she didn't have to answer the question herself.

Cole continued. "I have a question, too. How did you end up staying at the same motel we did?"

"No mystery there," Meg said. "My family always stays there when we're in El Paso. It's right off the highway, it has a restaurant, and it allows animals."

Cole nodded. "That's right—you mentioned that before." He glanced at Beau. "How did *you* show up so conveniently?"

"You left a message on Natty's voice mail."

"Oh, yeah, I forgot. And Meg thought she saw you pass us yesterday. I guess she was right, too. So, the only question left is, where's Baby?"

Meg glanced back at Jerry, to see him squirming.

Uh-oh. She had a feeling she wasn't going to like this. "What?"

"Uh, Baby's not in El Paso anymore."

"Why not?"

"The breeder was here on business, but he left just as soon as I turned Baby over to him."

"So, where's Baby now?"

"Tucson."

Tucson. Her spirits fell. Just when she thought things might be working out after all, Jerry had to throw another monkey wrench in the works.

Cole shrugged. "At least it's on the way to Phoenix. We'll still have time to find him before he has to be at the state fair."

We? Wait a minute...who invited him along? "What's this *we* stuff?"

Cole looked surprised. "I thought—"

"I don't need your help." Now that she had her truck back, she could drive to Tucson, pick up Baby and go on to Phoenix on her own. She was no longer in any danger from thieves, only from well-meaning but insensitive family members. Besides, Cole was just as bad as Jerry and Pops.

He glanced at her, but didn't answer. Instead, he pulled into the parking lot of the animal hospital.

Meg nodded when he didn't respond. Just as she'd expected. Good. She'd be better off on her own, anyway.

They parked and went inside. The receptionist gave them an odd look when four people trooped in to escort one small puppy, but merely asked them to wait. They seated themselves in the waiting room, and silence fell until Meg's name was called.

Cole followed her into the small examining room, and they fell into an uneasy silence, watching as Lady sniffed the examining table.

The vet joined them, a competent-looking older woman who immediately put Meg at ease. "What's the problem here?"

Cole took charge. "We're missing a rather large diamond ring, and we're afraid the puppy may have swallowed it."

"I see." The vet moved to the table and examined Lady, checking her teeth and ears and palpating her stomach. "Well, she seems to have eaten a lot of something. The only way to find out for sure if your ring is in there is to take an X ray."

He nodded. "That's what we thought. How long will it take?"

"Not too long—about twenty minutes." The vet glanced down at the puppy once more. "Has she had her shots?"

"I doubt it. We found her abandoned at a rest stop."

The vet nodded. "Well, it'll only take a couple of minutes to do that, too. Unless you'd rather wait for your own doctor?"

Cole turned to Meg, apparently finally remembering that Lady was supposed to be her dog.

"No, that's okay," she said. "We might as well get it done now."

As the vet prepared a syringe, Cole held Lady, stroking her fur and scratching her behind the ears to keep her calm. He murmured soft words of comfort as the vet pinched a fold of Lady's flesh and injected her.

Meg gazed at him in confusion. It was hard to reconcile the hard-bitten cop with the man who adored his son and treated small animals with such loving care. *Would the real Cole McKenzie please stand up?*

"There, that's done," the vet said. "If you'll leave her with me a few minutes, we'll take some X rays and let you know the results."

Meg nodded and followed Cole back into the waiting room, still confused. How could she reconcile Cole's contradictions? She shook her head. Right now, she didn't even want to try. She had enough problems as it was.

Beau looked up eagerly. "Did they find the ring?"

"Not yet," Meg said. "They're taking X rays now to see if she's eaten it."

Beau nodded, and his brow furrowed in thought. "If they find it, when can they perform the surgery?"

"Surgery?" What was he talking about?

"You know, to get the ring."

Meg gaped at him with what she was sure was a foolish expression, and Cole fielded the question. "The vet is not going to perform unnecessary surgery on a puppy just so you can get your ring back."

A sly grin came over Beau's face. "But you said yourself it's a large ring. What if it might harm the dog? Wouldn't they remove it then?"

Cole shrugged. "Maybe. But that's their call, not yours."

"But if they don't remove it, then how am I going to get it back?"

"The usual way, I suppose. You'll just have to wait for it to, er, come out the other end," Cole said.

Comprehension dawned on Beau's face, along with an expression of distaste. "You mean I'll have to follow the dog around, checking its...its..."

Cole grinned. "Yep. Unless you know a better way of doing it?"

"But...that could take a couple of days. I don't have that much time. I have to get the ring back to Mr. Peterson today." His gaze turned distant. "Maybe if I took the dog back with me..."

"Do you honestly think we'd let you?" Meg asked.

By now, even Jerry was giving Beau disgusted looks. "Why don't you just tell Peterson the situation?"

Beau glared at him. "Easy for you to say. Your job isn't on the line."

"You can't take her with you," Meg repeated. "You're just going to have to explain it to your boss. You're doing all you can to find the ring. Won't he understand?"

"I don't know. I doubt it."

"Well, you don't know until you try."

"But if I could just *borrow* the dog..."

"That's out of the question," Cole said. "And we don't even know if Lady swallowed it, anyway. Why don't we just wait until we find out what the doctor recommends?"

Beau sank into apathy, and Jerry followed him. Shortly thereafter, the vet came out and handed the puppy to Meg. "Well, we took the X rays and didn't find anything metallic. Looks like she didn't swallow the ring after all."

Beau's face fell. "Then where is it?"

Meg shrugged. "It must be back in the hotel room. We didn't look, remember? We just assumed Lady had eaten it."

Beau shot to his feet. "Okay, let's go."

He waited impatiently as they paid the bill and listened to the vet describe what the puppy would need over the next few months.

"Come on, come on," Beau muttered. He was almost jumping up and down in his haste to be gone.

Meg shot him an annoyed glance. "Don't worry. It'll still be there when we get back."

"Sure, sure..." Beau opened the door, hurrying them along when they didn't move fast enough for his taste. He even pestered Cole in the car on the way back to the motel, asking him to speed up. Meg grinned when Cole only went slower, which the distraught Beau didn't seem to notice.

"It's in the bathroom, it's in the bathroom, it's in the bathroom," Beau repeated over and over like a mantra.

When they finally reached the hotel, Beau bolted out of the car and ran to the room, then beat on the door. "Open up, Natty."

Natalie opened the door, and Beau rushed to the bathroom. "Noooooo..." he wailed for the second time.

Here we go again, Meg thought. "What's wrong this time?"

He swung around, wide-eyed. "Someone cleaned up the mess. Natty?" He shook his head. "No, of course you didn't. What am I thinking of?" He grabbed her arms. "Who cleaned?"

"The maid, of course. Who else? She vacuumed up the mess."

"Did she find the ring?"

Natalie glanced at the puppy. "I thought—"

"It's not in the dog, so it must have been in the bathroom. Did she mention finding something?" He broke off, shoving a hand through his hair. "No, of course she didn't. She probably found it and kept it. A seven-carat diamond ring—who wouldn't? Where is she now?"

"How would I know?" Natalie asked.

Annoyed by Beau's assumption that the maid was a thief, Meg said, "You don't know she took it. There was stuffing spread all over that room. Maybe she vacuumed it up by mistake."

"Right, right. Unless it's in the bedroom?" He turned to glance wildly around, then shook his head. "No, she would've vacuumed here, too. The vacuum. I need to find the vacuum."

"Then find the manager and ask to talk to the maid," Meg said in exasperation.

Beau's face brightened. "Right. Good idea. I'll call the manager."

He reached for the phone, but was stopped by Cole, who laid a restraining hand on the instrument. "We've had about enough of your accusations—and your damned ring. Go find the manager on your own."

Beau jerked his hand back and stared at it as if he were afraid he'd see nothing more than a stump. "Uh, sure. Right. I'll do that." He moved toward the door. "See you in a little bit, Natty."

He rushed out the door, not seeing the disgusted look Natalie threw at him.

Cole heaved a sigh and turned to Meg. "Well, now that we've gotten rid of Beau, we can continue on to Tucson to get Baby."

"I'm going with you," Natalie chimed in.

Meg recoiled. Having Cole, the two kids and a puppy in the car was bad enough, but Cole's ex-wife, too? That was an invitation to disaster.

Cole didn't look too thrilled about the idea, either. "Shouldn't you leave with Beau? You came with him, after all."

Natalie frowned. "I don't want to. He's dragged me all over Texas, and all he cares about is that stupid ring."

"Well, you can't come with us," Cole said.

"Us?" Meg repeated. "I told you before, I can do this on my own—or with Jerry." She slanted an angry look at her brother. "If he promises to behave."

Jerry cast her an indignant glance, but kept his mouth shut.

Cole gave her an odd look. "Can I talk to you a moment, privately?"

Meg nodded, and Cole drew her aside, out of earshot of the others. "Look, you need me."

Meg felt heat rising in her face. "What do you mean, I need you?"

"You need me to help you find Baby."

"I don't think so, Cole. Jerry will give me the breeder's address in Tucson. I think I can find it without your help. I can read a map, you know."

"But how are you going to convince the breeder that Baby is yours and Jerry sold him illegally?"

"I'll worry about that when I get there," she said, but Cole had a point. How *was* she going to convince the guy?

"I'm a cop," he reminded her. "I have a badge, and even though it's not any good in Arizona, it'll provide more credibility to your story."

Meg chewed her lip in thought, but didn't answer.

"You know I'm right," Cole said softly. "What is it you're really afraid of, Meg?"

Damn. That was the question she'd been avoiding. She was afraid of losing her dream, afraid of getting involved, afraid of what he was thinking.

How was she supposed to travel alone with him in the car, wondering about how he felt about her botched seduction the night before? If his ex-wife was any indication, Cole preferred the tall, willowy, sophisticated type, the kind who wore expensive clothes and expensive perfume—not a farm girl who smelled of rabbit dung.

He must have laughed at her clumsiness last night. Of course, he'd been polite enough not to let it show, but it was mortifying nonetheless.

"Meg?" Cole repeated. "What's wrong?"

Meg avoided his gaze. "Wrong? Oh, nothing. I'm just confused."

Boy, was that the understatement of the century! In all the romances she'd read, this was the part where the hero somehow divined the thoughts of the heroine, swept aside all her fears and doubts and assured her he loved her. Unfortunately, Cole didn't seem to be a mind reader. Then again, even if he was, her brother, his ex-wife, the two kids and the dog might cramp his style a bit.

Cole took her hands in his. "Look, it's simple. You need to get Baby back. I can help you. What's so confusing about that?"

True. The important thing was to get her dreams back on track, no matter how. And the best way to do that was to accept Cole's help to retrieve Baby. She sighed. "Okay. You can go with me."

She turned back to the room and spoke to Jerry. "Cole and I are taking the truck. You take the car and Susie back to Glenda."

Jerry frowned. "But I don't know anything about taking care of children."

"Well, Natalie's looking for a ride," Meg pointed out. "She can help with Susie." Come to think of it, there wasn't much room in the truck for the others. "And Luke and Lady, too."

"I don't think that's such a good idea," Cole said.

"Well, what do you suggest, then?" Meg asked in exasperation.

"Why don't we continue on to Tucson in Glenda's car, with Susie, Luke and Lady—and Natalie can go back to San Antonio with Jerry."

Natalie glanced at Jerry, a frown on her face. "But I don't even know him."

"Then you can stay and ride back with Beau."

Natalie's expression turned stubborn, and she gave Jerry an assessing look. Obviously she didn't want to go back with Beau but wasn't sure Jerry would be a fit companion.

"Hey, lady," Jerry said. "You don't have to ride with me if you don't want to. Besides, I'm not going to San Antonio just yet. I've decided to go on to Phoenix." He gave Meg a sheepish look. "Once Meg gets the rabbit back, my future's riding on the judging at that fair."

Natalie still appeared doubtful, so Meg intervened. "It's okay," she assured the other woman. "Jerry's harmless. If you're not a rabbit or a race car, he won't even notice you exist."

Natalie's eyes lit up. "Race car? You race cars? How interesting."

Jerry looked surprised at her interest. "Sure. I'm getting pretty good, too. Just won a local championship."

"But isn't that ... dangerous?"

Dangerous? Boring and inane was more like it. Hot, dirty, smelly racetracks were not Meg's idea of fun.

He shrugged. "Sometimes."

Natalie patted his arm. "Good. You can tell me all about it on the way to Phoenix ... if the offer still holds?"

Jerry beamed, flattered by the attention. "Sure. Why not?"

Natalie stood and grabbed her purse. "All right, let's go, then. I want to be gone before Beau gets back. I'll just leave him a note and we can be on our way, okay?"

Jerry grinned. "Okay."

Meg looked at Cole to see how he was taking this, but he just shook his head. "So," he said, "shall we go, too?"

Meg sighed. "I guess so." She wasn't crazy about being there when Beau got back, either. *If* he came back. He was so single-minded that she wouldn't put it past him to just take off without a word to the rest of them after he found the ring.

Then again, who cared?

Jerry turned over the check and Baby's papers to Meg, along with her suitcase, and he and Natalie waved as they drove off in the truck.

Cole turned to Meg. "You ready to go?"

"Whenever you are." The sooner they got going, the sooner she'd be able to fulfill her dream.

BEAU HURRIED to the check-in desk to find the maid. He was finally zeroing in on the diamond, and he didn't have a moment to lose. If he had his hands on the ring, he could call Mr. Peterson and let him know it was coming.

Maybe his boss *would* understand. After all, Beau was an excellent employee. Of course, he'd only been working there a short while, but he'd proved himself. He was a damned good salesman, and Mr. Peterson had to know that. Surely he'd give him the benefit of the doubt if he had the ring in hand.

Beau approached the counter with more confidence. He explained the situation to the man behind the desk, though the guy couldn't seem to get it through his head why Beau wanted to talk to the maid. Beau finally made him understand, and he called in the maid who'd cleaned the room.

The young girl came in and rubbed her hands down the side of her skirt. Good—she was nervous. Nervous people betrayed themselves more easily and were more apt to make mistakes.

Beau smiled and took her hand. "Hello. What's your name?"

The girl smiled back. "Rosa."

"Rosa? That's a beautiful name," he said in a soothing voice and stroked her hand. "Rosa, I hope you can help me."

She moved her head in a nervous gesture and gave him a half smile.

"Rosa," he repeated, because he knew people enjoyed hearing their own names. It put them at ease. "Do you remember cleaning room 126?"

She wrinkled her brow in puzzlement. "I'm not sure...."

"The one with the lady and two children in it, with a very messy bathroom?"

She nodded, more confident now.

"Did you find anything in the bathroom, Rosa? Besides the mess, I mean?"

She shook her head. "I don't think so."

"Think about it, please. This is very important."

As she thought some more, Beau studied her face. Either she really hadn't seen the diamond, or she was a good enough actress to fool him. No, she couldn't be that good. Now what? Could it be in the vacuum?

"I don't remember anything," she said. "What are you looking for?"

"My fiancée lost her engagement ring, and she's frantic to get it back."

"Oh, that's awful."

That was the right tack to take—he had her feeling sorry for him. "Do you think you might have vacuumed it up by mistake?"

She shrugged. "Maybe. We can go look if you like."

"Thank you, Rosa, that would be wonderful."

Satisfied with himself, Beau strolled out the door after the maid. This was more like it. Finally, someone was cooperating with him.

She retrieved the vacuum cleaner, and he followed her to an empty room, where she disconnected the bag and handed it to him.

"What's this for?" he asked.

"You wanted to search the vacuum. Here. This is it."

"But I thought you . . ."

Her look turned cool. "It's your ring, not mine. If you want to find it, you can look through here." She shrugged. "Or not. Your choice."

Frowning, he grabbed the bag away from her and dumped its contents on the floor.

"Hey, wait a minute!" she cried. "You're making a mess!"

"Well, how else am I going to find out what's in here?"

She scowled at him. "Well, then, you can clean it up when you're finished." She flounced out of the room.

Beau stared down at the debris in disgust and sneezed. Luckily, the bag had only been half-full, but there was still a lot of junk to dig through. He knew he had the right one, though, because he recognized the stuffing.

Gingerly he picked out a plastic eye and what looked like a pink nose. Yep, definitely bunny parts.

Thirty minutes later, he and the room were covered with dust from one end to the other. He stared down at himself in distaste. He'd found plenty of dust, sand and fuzzy rabbit parts... but no ring. His thoughts turned frantic, and he broke out in a cold sweat. Where could it be?

If it wasn't here, then it must be in the hotel room. He just hadn't searched thoroughly enough. Maybe it was in the bedroom. That was it—now all he had to do was find it.

Eagerly he leaped up and ran to the room to pound on the door.

No answer. He pounded harder. "Natty!" he cried. "Let me in!" Still no answer.

Damn. Had they checked out? He backed up to peer in the window and found a note pinned to the door with his name on it. He jerked it off the door and read it.

Beau, don't bother looking for me, or seeing me ever again. I've gone to the Arizona State Fair with the others. I hope you find your ring. Natalie.

Beau crumpled the note in his fist, and his eyes narrowed. She hoped he found the ring? What did she think he was...stupid? There was no way Natty would leave him. Especially not when he'd hinted strongly that he planned to propose. There had to be another reason.

The ring...that was it. They'd found the ring and had headed off to Arizona with it, laughing up their sleeves at him. Well, he could play that little game, too. He'd just follow them to Phoenix and then see who had the last laugh.

Chapter Eight

They'd passed the state line early and were now in New Mexico, still on the same monotonous road. Cole glanced at Meg. She'd been quiet an awful long time. Her vitality was muted, as if someone had put a damper on it. What was wrong?

The children were playing quietly in the back seat, and would be fine for a while. Now was his opportunity to talk to her and figure out what was going through her head. As she stared out the window, Cole said, "Meg?"

"Hmm?"

"Are you all right?"

She shrugged.

"There's something bothering you. Is it something I did?"

"No, no. Not you."

If it wasn't him, then it must be... "Jerry?"

She grimaced. "And Pops."

Damn. He wasn't very good at this, but it seemed like she needed someone to talk to. "Do you want to talk about it?"

"I don't know...I haven't really had anyone to talk to since Gram died."

He grinned at her. "Well, just pretend I'm your grandmother, then, and tell me all your troubles."

She cast him a sidelong look. "My, my, Grandma, what big...pecs you have."

He chuckled. "The better to comfort you with, my dear." Unfortunately, she didn't look comforted, so he said, "Talking might help."

She sighed and said, "I guess so. It's just..."

"Just that you want them to treat you as a human being."

"I suppose so." She paused, then said, "Yeah, that's right. They didn't even think how I would feel when they stole my truck and my rabbit. They just took them away from me like I didn't matter."

"Do you think that's how they really feel?" He didn't want to judge—that was up to her to decide.

"No, they just...take me for granted."

"Dependable old Meg," he said softly.

Her lower lip quivered, and he berated himself. He hadn't meant to make her cry.

"I'm so *tired* of that!" she wailed, and wiped tears from her eyes. "I want people to look at me as something other than someone they can kick around whenever they want to, like a...like a..."

He sought for something to lighten the atmosphere. "Like an old sock?"

She chuckled despite herself. "A what?"

At least it had worked. Her tears had dried up. "Oh, sorry, wrong analogy. I mean an old shoe."

She sobered, but still wore a smile on her face. "Yeah, an old shoe. I'm really tired of that."

"So, why let them?"

"How can I stop them?"

"You could start by saying no."

"What do you mean?"

"Well, when they ask you to organize the sock hop, baby-sit twelve kids, run the entire firemen's muster or serve tea and crumpets to the governor, just say no."

"It's not that easy," she mumbled.

"No, really, it is," he assured her. "Try it. Two little letters, one small syllable. No. Nnnnn... Ohhhh... Now you try it."

She drawled the letters after him.

"Okay, now put the two sounds together. Nnnnooo..."

"No," she repeated.

"That was great. Now try it again until you become comfortable with it.

"No," she said tentatively, then more strongly. "No. No. No, no, no, no, no, *no*."

Luke and Susie echoed her from the back seat, until a veritable chorus of naysayers echoed through the car.

Cole chuckled. "See how easy it is?"

Meg laughed, and Cole raised his voice to say, "Okay, kids, that's enough."

The kids quieted down and went back to playing, giving Cole the opportunity to continue probing. "So, have you ever thought about leaving Pops and Jerry behind and striking out on your own?"

"I've thought about it, but Gram made me promise before she died that I'd ensure they were taken care of."

"But that doesn't mean *you* have to be the one to do it, does it?"

"If not me, then who?"

"Doesn't Jerry have a girlfriend? Or Pops?"

She shook her head.

"How about hiring someone to clean house, cook meals and remind your grandfather to take his medication?"

She shook her head again, biting her lip. "That wouldn't work."

"Why not?" Cole asked in a gentle tone. "Because you're not sure anyone else could take care of them as well as you?" He met her frown with an unflinching stare. "That's it, isn't it?"

"Maybe. But they couldn't afford a housekeeper, anyway."

"Of course they can't—and they won't. Why should they, when you're there to do all the work for them. Maybe if you weren't around, they wouldn't take you for granted anymore."

"Maybe," she repeated, and appeared lost in thought.

"And even if you win the bet and move to San Antonio, how will things be different? They'll still want you to take care of them, even in the city."

"I don't know," Meg said in a small voice.

Cole left her alone with her thoughts as he continued driving through the desert, figuring he'd given her enough to think about. She had a tough time ahead of her, if she was going to reconcile her desire for excitement with her need to take care of her family—the two just weren't compatible. But *she'd* have to worry about that. He'd complicated things enough by asking the question in the first place.

She was quiet for a long time, but Luke and Susie more than made up for it, as their play in the back seat turned noisy. Meg turned to them—gratefully, Cole thought—to sing and play road games and generally keep the kids calmed down. He wasn't sure whether she was doing it to keep the little ones occupied or to avoid talking to him, but no matter what her reason, it accomplished both.

They stopped in Lordsburg for lunch at a fast-food restaurant again because of the puppy, and ate their hamburgers and fries, enjoying being out of the car for a change. As the kids worked off their high spirits by horsing around with the dog, Cole glanced at Meg, who sipped her soda and watched them play.

He grinned. She'd been so conscientious about the children that she hadn't taken care of herself. He leaned over the table to get her attention. "You've got mustard on your face."

She looked up at him in surprise. "Where?" Her tongue flicked out to each corner of her mouth, then circled her lips in an innocent gesture that set his blood boiling.

He couldn't help it—his gaze riveted on her tongue and he felt himself grow hard. Some of his arousal must have communicated itself to Meg, for she stilled, her tongue frozen in the act of licking her lips.

"No," he said in a voice that had become husky. "Here." He reached across the table and wiped the smear of mustard from her cheek. He couldn't help lingering over the movement, turning it into an unintentional caress.

She shut her mouth abruptly and pulled away, averting her gaze.

"Meg," he said softly. "What's wrong?"

Her cheeks flushed. "I— You— Last night—"

"It's okay," he assured her in a soothing voice. "What about last night?"

"I don't usually..."

Though she'd pulled her face away, her arm was still within easy reach, so he stroked it, wanting to touch her, to feel her soft skin. "Don't you think I know that?" Oh, she'd tried to act like an experienced seductress, but her innocence was obvious.

She shrugged and wouldn't meet his gaze, but...she didn't pull her arm away, not even when he moved his fingers to trace circles on the back of her hand.

She had no reason to be embarrassed, though she undoubtedly was. He knew how these things went— she'd started out wanting the excitement and titillation of experiencing the most intimate relationship between a man and a woman, but ended up being frightened by those feelings. How could he convince her that her feelings were normal, and that she shouldn't be embarrassed?

"What do you say we start over?" he asked.

"Start over?"

"Yes." He smiled and curled his fingers into hers. "Would you go out with me tonight?"

She blushed and gazed at their entwined fingers. "You mean, like a...date?"

He tipped her chin so that he could look her in the eyes. "Yes, like a date."

She glanced at the children and Lady. "For five?"

"No, just you and me."

"But how?"

At least she wasn't saying no. "I'll find a baby-sitter to watch them while we go out. What do you say?"

She smiled then—a shy curving of her lips that spoke eloquently of her innocence. "All right. Yes."

Inside, Cole exulted, but he forced himself to respond calmly. "Good. Then the sooner we get going, the sooner we can find Baby and get started on our date."

FROM LORDSBURG, it was only a few miles to the Arizona state line, and a couple hours more to Tucson. They stopped at a gas station for directions to Jackson Murphy's place—he was the breeder who had bought Baby—and soon found themselves driving up to a prosperous-looking farmhouse with several outbuildings.

"This must be the place," Meg said. "He has the right setup."

She was more relieved than she cared to admit. Now that she'd seen the man's place, she had more confidence in his ability to take care of Baby.

Cole shut off the engine. "How do you plan on handling this?"

"What do you mean?"

"I assume you're planning on telling the truth?"

"Yes, of course. What else?"

"Then you're planning to ask for his cooperation and count on his good nature to turn the rabbit over to you?"

"Well, yes." What other way was there to go about it?

"What if he won't? What if he refuses?"

"I . . . I don't know. I hadn't thought about it."

"Well, I have. And I think it might be best if you stayed in the car with the kids while I approach him to see how he's going to react."

"Why? You're not going to . . . beat him up or anything, are you?"

He raised one eyebrow. "No, I don't usually beat up total strangers to get my jollies."

"But what can you say to him that I can't?" If she was going to be the new, adventurous Meg Hollingsworth, she might as well start here and now.

He gave her an exasperated glance. "Look, Meg. You're an innocent, and it shows all over your face. If he's unscrupulous, he might try to take advantage of you. He won't with me."

She nodded, but persisted. "But it's *my* rabbit."

"True, and if everything seems fine, I'll call you over to talk to him about it. Otherwise, I'll take care of it my way. Okay?"

"Okay," she said reluctantly. Some adventure this was turning out to be, if all she did was sit in the car and baby-sit.

She watched as he approached the house and knocked on the door. Soon, a woman came to the door. Cole had a short conversation with her, then left.

He got back in the car and faced Meg.

"What happened?" she asked.

"Well, he's not there."

"Baby's not there?" she asked on a note of rising panic. "What have they done with him?"

"No, no. I mean Murphy's not there. He hasn't made it back from El Paso yet, because he had other business. His wife doesn't expect him back until late tonight."

Her shoulders slumped. "Terrific. Now what?"

"Now we wait, and come back tomorrow morning, when he'll be here. His wife will tell him to expect us."

"Did you tell her about Baby?"

"No, I didn't see any reason to—I just told her we needed to talk to him about his breeding program."

She nodded. "But that means we have to stay in Tucson tonight."

He grinned and started the car. "Yep. And I know just the place."

He stopped at a phone booth to make a call and got back in the car, grinning. "It's all set up. You're not the only one with cousins, you know."

"Cousins?"

"My cousin Jim lives here in Tucson with his wife, Carol, and their three kids. I haven't seen them in a while, and they're more than willing to let us stay with them for the night."

"That's nice of them," she said, glad to hear she wouldn't have to stretch her money to cover another hotel room.

Cole grinned wickedly at her. "Not only that, but they've agreed to baby-sit, so you and I can have a night out alone."

A feeling of warmth spread throughout her body as she contemplated the evening ahead. Cole was going to a great deal of trouble to make sure they had some time alone and could enjoy themselves. No one else had ever done so much for her. "Are you sure they don't mind?"

"No, believe me, it's no problem," he assured her. "Ever since my divorce, my family's been trying to fix me up with one woman or another, but I've resisted all their efforts. This time I saved them the trouble."

Meg's heart beat a muted thump-thump-thump inside her rib cage. So it had been a while since he'd been out with a woman. What did that mean? Was she up to the challenge of being the first woman he'd dated since Natalie? Meg recalled the willowy model and wondered how she could ever compete with *that*.

She didn't have long to worry, because Cole soon pulled into the driveway of an older house in an upscale neighborhood.

The door opened, and a thirtyish-looking couple came out to greet them, followed by three young children.

Jim, a slender, blond version of Cole, thumped him on the back while Carol, a plump brunette with a wide smile, gave him a fierce hug. "It's been so long since we've seen you," she exclaimed. She turned her smile on Meg. "Hi, I'm Carol."

"And I'm Jim," the man said, with a smile as big as his wife's.

Meg held out her hand, but they ignored it and reached out to hug her as if they'd been family for years. After a moment of surprise, Meg hugged them back. Why not? She wanted to be more of a spontaneous free spirit, and that meant hugging people, didn't it? Besides, these two McKenzies were so open and effusive in their welcome that they made Meg feel at home right away.

As they all went into the house—the four adults, five children and one dog—the house resounded with merriment. Meg smiled, basking in the emotion. This must be what Cole had meant when he spoke of growing up surrounded by love and laughter. It was a great feeling, especially after being raised by her rather laconic and taciturn grandfather. Did Cole have any idea how lucky he was to have a family like this?

She glanced at him then, and he returned the glance with a grin and a question in his eyes. She grinned back and nodded. This was great. Apparently reassured, Cole went to join Jim in the living room, while Carol steered Meg into the bright, airy kitchen.

"Would you like some iced tea?" Carol asked.

Meg seated herself at the kitchen table. "That sounds wonderful."

Carol handed her a glass of tea and poured one for herself, then joined Meg. "So, I understand you two would like a little time for yourselves this evening." Her gaze was bright and questioning.

Meg nodded, already feeling as if she'd known this woman most of her life. "That's right. We've been riding in the car for two days, and Cole thought it might be a good idea for us to have some time away from the kids.''

''How long have you known each other?'' Though Carol's question was direct, she didn't seem disapproving, just genuinely curious.

''Since yesterday.''

Carol seemed a bit taken aback at that. ''Yesterday? But the way you two looked at each other, I thought...''

Meg's cheeks heated with embarrassment. Were her feelings that obvious? ''No, we met yesterday morning, when he helped me chase after my rabbit.'' She explained the situation, saying, ''We've been together ever since.''

''So you've been with Cole now for more than twenty-four hours?''

Meg nodded.

Carol gave her a knowing smile. ''That's more than enough time to fall for one of these McKenzie boys. I should know—it only took me five minutes to fall for Jim.''

Meg's heart flipped over. Was that what was happening to her? Was she falling for Cole? She ducked her head, not certain how to respond to Carol's statement.

Carol's voice was soft, compassionate. ''You *have* fallen for him, haven't you?''

''I—I'm not sure. How can you tell?''

''Well, do you get light-headed whenever he's near? And you feel tingly when he touches you?''

Meg nodded.

"And does your stomach kind of churn and lurch whenever you think about him?"

Meg settled a hand on her stomach. Like now? "Yes, but that sounds more like the flu."

Carol chuckled. "Yep. Unfortunately, the symptoms are the same."

Meg grimaced. She wasn't sure she liked the idea of falling in love with Cole. He was supposed to be her exciting fling, her one-night stand, not the love of her life. He didn't seem the happily-ever-after type. "When does it stop?"

"Oh, it never really stops, it just settles down to a more manageable and comfortable level, once you realize he's got the same symptoms."

That was what was making Meg uneasy. "How can I tell if he does?" And did she really want to know?

Carol patted her on the arm in a consoling gesture. "You can't, unless he tells you. And he probably won't. Men are like that."

"So how did *you* know?" This was a new experience for Meg, and she needed all the help she could get.

"Well, I wasn't sure until Jim actually told me he loved me and asked me to marry him."

Meg's shoulders slumped. Marriage. She'd started this adventure to avoid that. It wasn't what she was looking for, and she didn't think Cole was, either, since his first one hadn't worked out.

Carol patted her on the arm again. "But don't worry—there are other signs. If he kisses you in public, constantly finds ways to touch you in small ways, things like that, then it's a good sign he's smitten."

Well, he hadn't kissed her much, but today, he had touched her more than seemed normal. Hope dawned in her chest. "Do you think..."

Carol grinned. "It's possible. In fact, I'd say downright probable, judging from the look he gave you earlier."

She wanted to be honest with her new friend. "But I'm not sure I want to be in love with him—or have him in love with me."

Carol laughed. "Honey, if you get involved with one of the McKenzie boys, you may not have a choice." She turned serious. "But if you want to keep your heart whole and fancy-free, don't let him take you to bed, or you'll be a goner for sure."

Meg blushed and averted her gaze. She definitely wanted him to take her to bed. But... was it worth falling in love?

Carol checked her watch. "And if you want to have dinner out, you'd better start getting ready. Do you have something to change into?"

Meg brightened. Now that she'd retrieved her suitcase, she did have something to wear. She'd packed a brand-new party dress, just in case she had an occasion like this to wear it. Eagerly she fetched the suitcase from the car and took it inside.

Carol insisted Meg take a long, luxurious bubble bath while she supervised the kids. Meg took full advantage of the offer and soaked for a good hour while she let her mind roam over possible scenarios for the evening.

Carol had made it clear that the choice of beds was up to Meg, and that she could share one with Cole in the guest house—or not—when they got back. It was totally up to her.

Being in Cole's arms seemed an appropriate way to provide the excitement she longed for, but if she was in danger of losing her heart to him, as Carol had indicated, was it worth it?

Well, Meg decided as she got out of the tub, she didn't have to decide that until much later this evening.

She dried off, then picked up the striking emerald green silk shantung dress she'd bought about a month ago. She'd never worn it, and wasn't sure she'd have the nerve to.

It looked demure enough in front, with its short sleeves, high mandarin collar and small keyhole opening just below the throat, but the back was positively sinful. The opening there started at the neck and widened to expose her shoulder blades and leave her entire back bare, until it closed again in a V right below her waist.

She slipped into it and checked out her reflection. It wasn't something she normally would've bought, but the saleslady had been adamant that this dress was perfect for her and assured Meg that she had a beautiful back that was just made for it.

She'd been persuaded then, but now she was a little nervous. Wearing a bra and panty hose was out of the question in this dress, and it made her look—and feel—a little wanton, as if she were someone else.

She took a deep breath. That was what she wanted, wasn't it? To feel like someone else? Someone daring, provocative, sexy? Well, with this dress she fit the daring part, anyway.

Nervously she began applying her makeup, but then she heard a knock at the door.

"Meg, can I come in?" Carol called.

Meg opened the door and Carol said, "Don't worry. The guys are off in the other room, so it's just you and me."

She nodded and turned back to the mirror.

Carol's eyes widened. "Holy cow."

Meg met her gaze in the mirror. "Do you think it's too much?"

Carol chuckled, a deep, mischievous laugh that started in her chest and burst full-throated from her lips. "Oh, no. It's just right. Cole won't know what hit him."

Meg fumbled with her eye shadow and Carol said, "Here, let me help. I've had some experience with this stuff after living with three sisters."

Meg let Carol make her up and fiddle with her hair. She didn't figure there was much that could be done with her unruly curls, but Carol managed to tame them a little bit and swept one side up in a style that even Meg thought made her look sophisticated.

When she was done, Meg put on a pair of flats, and Carol frowned. "That dress would look much better with heels."

"But I don't have any with me."

"What size do you wear?"

Meg told her and Carol grinned. "Great. We're the same size. Hold on." She dug in the closet and brought out a pair of black high-heeled sandals. "Here, try these on."

Meg slipped them on and teetered for a moment. "I don't know—I'm not used to wearing heels."

"You'll be fine—just walk slowly and you won't have any problems. Come here." Carol pulled Meg over in front of the full-length mirror. "See how fabulous you look?"

Meg gaped, not recognizing the person who stared back at her. This woman was everything Meg wanted to be...or at least she *looked* like everything Meg wanted to be. She'd already achieved daring, and with Carol's help, she thought, maybe she might have hit upon provocative and sexy, too.

Carol stood next to her and grinned. "Like I said, Cole won't know what hit him. He's ready—why don't we go knock his socks off?"

Meg wiped her damp palms on a nearby towel, so as not to soil her dress, then followed Carol out of the room.

Cole and Jim were in the living room, chatting while the kids watched television. As Meg and Carol entered, they rose to their feet.

Cole had changed into dark gray slacks and a white shirt with a conservative tie and blazer. She'd thought he was sexy in blue jeans and a T-shirt, but this made him look positively gorgeous—dark and dangerous.

He had a stunned expression on his face that Meg found particularly gratifying. He didn't say anything, he just stood there with his mouth half-open and a dumbstruck look on his face. Meg darted a hesitant glance at Carol, who grinned and gave her a thumbs-up.

Meg managed to smile, and Luke broke the silence. The little boy looked up at her with his mouth half-open in unconscious imitation of his dad's and said, "Wow, Aunt Meg *pretty*."

The adults all laughed, and it seemed to break the trance Cole had fallen into. "That's right, sport," he said. "Meg is pretty, isn't she?" He grinned as Jim slapped him on the back. "And I get her all to myself tonight." He smiled to Meg. "Shall we go?"

Meg nodded and turned to precede him out the door. Before she could take another step, she heard a sharply indrawn breath. She glanced over her shoulder at Cole and saw the poleaxed look reappear as his gaze drifted down the curve of her back. Jim and Carol shared an amused glance.

Cole recovered and placed a warm hand at the small of her back. "Did I say pretty?" he murmured into her ear as they walked out the door. "I meant sensational."

Meg faltered. The combination of his hand spread intimately against her skin and his warm breath teasing the strands of hair on her neck was making her light-headed, almost as if she were floating somewhere above the scene.

As they approached the car, Cole placed a soft kiss on the side of her neck, and Meg almost melted with the sheer pleasure of it. Was she ready for this?

She swallowed hard. No, but she was damned well going to experience it anyway.

Chapter Nine

Meg glanced around in appreciation as Cole escorted her into Henri's. Warm lighting cast a glow over the rich burgundy-and-gold furnishings as quiet conversations mixed with the soft strains of a piano. The overall ambience was one of romance and lush opulence...the mood, hushed expectancy. She shivered in anticipation.

The maitre d' took one look at Cole's possessive hand on Meg's waist and seated them in a curved alcove at a table elegantly set for two. It allowed them a view of the room, but felt secluded, intimate.

Too intimate—it scared Meg to death. She was excited, yes, but she hadn't expected to experience terror at the same time. How was she going to handle this evening without becoming sick?

She felt totally inadequate. In his dark sport coat and white shirt against tanned skin, Cole was drop-dead gorgeous—any woman's idea of a dream date. She'd seen plenty of women's heads turning as they came in, and she couldn't blame them. What did *he* see in *her*?

"...would you like?" Cole said, glancing up from a small menu.

"Uh, what?"

"Would you like something to drink? Wine, perhaps?"

"I don't drink much, but—" she decided to be daring "—this is a night for new experiences. Wine sounds good. You decide."

The amber wine sparkled and shimmered in the candlelight as the waiter poured it into the crystal and offered it to Cole. Cole sipped, his dark, brooding eyes never leaving hers.

Meg dragged her gaze away and picked up the dinner menu. She stared at it unseeingly for several minutes, trying to bring her wayward emotions under control. Her heart was beating like a tom-tom, booming out her fear that she was going to make an utter fool of herself.

"Do you see anything you like?" Cole asked.

See anything? She hadn't been able to focus on a single word. "I... I'm not sure. Why don't you order for me? Anything's fine." Especially since she wasn't sure she'd be able to swallow a bite, anyway.

"All right." Cole turned back to the menu and perused it with a thoughtful air, then ordered.

The waiter left, and the remains of Meg's self-confidence left with him. Now that they were alone, what was she supposed to do? She gave Cole a desperate glance, hoping for a clue.

He raised his eyebrow and his glass to her. "A toast?"

Oh, good. Something to do. She granted him what had to be a sick-looking smile and raised her glass in return. "To what?"

"To...dreams. And fulfilling them."

"To dreams," she murmured, and sipped her wine. It was better than she'd expected, with a light, delicate flavor that went down smoothly.

"Very good," she said, and took another sip to keep herself occupied. The third swallow sent a marvelous calming sensation washing through her that made her muscles unclench and her bones turn light and airy.

She sighed. Feeling a little less strained, Meg smiled at Cole. He gazed back with those seductive bedroom eyes of his, and her pulse leaped in response. She placed a hand over her heart, wishing it would stop doing that.

Cole leaned closer, moving so that he could sit next to her in the curved booth, and gazed into her eyes. "You seem a little nervous."

She took another sip. "I am...a little."

He trailed his fingers along her forearm. "No need to be. It's just me, Cole. The same guy you've spent the last two days with...the same guy who helped you clean up after kids and puppies..."

He tipped her chin up to gaze at her with a sexy half smile that made her heart turn over in her breast. "The same guy whose shirt you borrowed...and the same guy you slept with last night."

She blushed and averted her gaze. How could he remind her of that?

"Come on, Meg," he murmured in her ear. "It wasn't that bad. See, this is the same shirt. No damage to it—or to you." His voice dropped to a husky whisper. "And just like last night, nothing will happen unless you want it to."

Meg nodded, but still wouldn't meet his eyes. She was too embarrassed. She'd failed at her one and only seduction attempt, and she didn't know whether she had the nerve to try again.

Cole shifted away slightly. "So. What would you like to do after dinner? Go home, see a movie, dance?"

"Dance?" She glanced out at the small dance floor, where several couples were swaying to soft music. "I'd love to dance."

"Then dance it is," Cole said. "What kind of music do you like?"

With that, he turned the conversation to the less personal. Over dinner, they discussed music, movies and books, and took a stab at solving the world's problems. Through it all, Meg was ever conscious of Cole's body close to her own, his leg pressed intimately against hers, and an ever-expanding sense of well-being.

She didn't remember what she ate, she only knew it was delicious. And though she had two glasses of wine, she was relieved to discover that she didn't feel intoxicated, just relaxed. By the time dinner was finished, she was very mellow, and more than ready to experience the heady delights the night might bring.

Cole smiled at her. "Would you like to dance now?"

Meg nodded and let Cole lead her to the dance floor.

As the band played a slow, sensuous song, she melted into his embrace. Cole held her snugly against him, his hand warm on the bare skin of her back and the other holding her hand cuddled in his.

A feeling of contentment washed over her. Here in Cole's arms, she felt warm and cherished. She hesitated for a moment. Warm and cherished? Wasn't that what she'd been trying to avoid?

Cole murmured reassurances and pulled her closer against his lean, hard frame. His caress against her back was slow, exquisite, and entirely bewitching.

Avoid this? Not a chance. This warm and cherished feeling came with a healthy side helping of sensuality that she definitely wanted to experience.

As she relaxed once again in Cole's arms, he pulled her close and spun her around the dance floor in dizzying circles of sensation. The feelings mirrored the swirls of desire that started from the base of her spine and slowly insinuated themselves throughout the most private recesses of her body.

She'd thought the wine intoxicating, but it was nothing compared to the emotions Cole aroused in her. The music stopped, and he gazed at her with a question in his eyes. With a sigh, Meg laid her head on his shoulder, wanting to prolong this magic moment as long as possible.

The music resumed, and so did their slow dance of seduction. She tried to identify each one of the delicious sensations spiraling through her body, but had trouble telling excitement from anticipation... or fear... or pure desire.

The music changed, becoming slower, more enthralling, until it filled her. Cole pressed a light kiss against her neck and her senses spun into overdrive, leaving her dizzy with a strange, unspoken need. She glanced up at him, wordlessly, her lips parted in surprise and instinctive invitation.

Cole responded by pressing his lips against hers in a tender, exploratory caress. He raised his head to search her face, and she licked her lips and gazed at him in anticipation, silently begging him to do it again.

He did, capturing her mouth in a long, lingering kiss that took her breath away. She coiled her fist into the curls at the back of his neck, reveling in the silky feel of his hair against her fingers, and succumbed to the giddy feeling of being in his arms.

An eon later, Cole released her, murmuring, "The music's stopped."

She gazed up at him, but didn't let go. "So it has."

He gave her another soft kiss. "I think we'd better continue this elsewhere, before we provide entertainment for half of Tucson."

At this point, Meg didn't care. The evening had gone wonderfully so far. It looked like she was halfway to getting her wish fulfilled, and she wanted to go all the way—to have a night she'd remember the rest of her life.

She sighed. Unfortunately, that meant she'd have to let go of Cole for a few moments. "All right," she said. "Let me visit the rest room first. After all, I haven't seen my share of strange bathrooms yet today."

Cole chuckled, and Meg headed off toward the ladies' room while he paid the check. She hurried back as fast as she could, but an older man with a slight paunch stopped her as she came out of the bathroom.

"Hey, girlie," he slurred, laying a meaty hand on her arm. "Ya wanna dance?"

"No, thank you," she said, and tried to pull her arm away.

No such luck. He held it in a crushing grip. "C'mon, jus' one li'l little dance."

"No," she said more forcefully, and tried to pry his hand off with her other hand. "I'm leaving. Let go of me."

He grabbed both arms then and shoved his beery face into hers. "Whatsa matter? Not good 'nuff for you?"

She saw Cole come up behind the man, and her eyes widened at the murderous look on Cole's face. Damn, how did she get herself into these situations? She didn't want to cause any trouble—and she certainly didn't want *Cole* to, either—but from the expression on his face, trouble was already front and center.

Imagining all the worst barroom brawls she'd seen in the movies, Meg cringed and her stomach clenched in automatic rejection. *No,* she wailed to herself—this was not how she wanted to end her perfect night.

Cole tapped her tormentor on the shoulder, and the guy swung his face around. Meg flinched, expecting Cole to punch him right then and there, but he surprised her.

"Excuse me," Cole said, "but that's my date you have there."

"Oh, yeah?"

"Yeah. And I'd like her back now." His voice was amiable, but his expression brooked no argument.

The man's grip loosened as he gave Cole an incredulous glance. "You would, huh?"

"Yes, I would." Cole lowered his voice to a menacing tone that sounded like the growl of an angry panther. "Let her go... now."

The guy was several inches taller than Cole and had at least forty pounds on him, but Cole clearly had the edge. The man must have thought so, too, for he looked quickly at Cole, then at Meg, who gave him a tight smile.

"You'd better do as he says," she whispered. "You don't want to know what Rambo did to the last guy who touched me."

Panic lit the man's eyes for a moment, and he released her. He staggered off, muttering, "Sorry, wrong girl."

Cole escorted her out the door, his hand warm on her back, and leaned down to whisper in her ear, "Rambo, huh?"

She gave him a fleeting glance, and was glad to see amusement brimming in his gaze. She shrugged. "You looked so tough that it just popped out. He must've thought so, too, 'cause he sure let go of me quick enough."

Cole chuckled and steered her toward the car, hesitating before opening the door. "He didn't hurt you, did he?"

She rubbed her upper arms. "No."

He cupped her cheek in his hand and gave her a gentle peck on the mouth. "I'm glad you weren't hurt. You looked so scared, but I wasn't sure if you were more scared of him . . . or me."

"Neither was I," she admitted. "I was afraid you were going to flatten him."

He kissed her on the wrist. "Ah, now you're mixing me up with Rambo again."

"Yes, I think I am," she said softly. "Thank you."

"For what?"

"For not being Rambo. For not spoiling our special evening."

"You're welcome," he murmured. Then a hesitant look crossed his face. "Is it over already?"

Her heart turned over at this evidence of his uncertainty, and any doubts she'd had melted away. Just this one night, she'd let Cole love her, cherish her, then watch him leave without a single regret.

She bestowed what she hoped was a seductive smile on him and ran her hand up his chest, pausing in puzzlement when she heard something crackle in the breast pocket of his shirt. "What's that?"

Cole shrugged and reached in his pocket to pull out a small package. Oh no—the condom she'd secreted there the night before, when *she* wore the shirt.

He held it up and gave her a questioning look. Meg felt her face turn hot and knew her fair skin gave her away. She gulped and tried for an nonchalant air. "Well, I see you're prepared for the rest of the night, anyway."

Cole laughed and tucked the condom back into his shirt pocket, then gave her a swift, hot kiss filled with tantalizing promises.

Meg kissed him back just as fiercely, glad that she'd let her inhibitions go for one night. She had a feeling it would be worth it.

THE DRIVE back to Jim and Carol's house was one of the longest Cole had ever taken. He didn't remember how they got into the guest house—all he knew was that he wanted to be there with Meg more than anything else in the world.

He shut the door behind them and turned the light on, watching her for some clue to her feelings. She shifted uncomfortably, and her hands and gaze fluttered about like frightened birds, looking for something, anything, to land on.

The guest house was really nothing more than an efficiency apartment. Her gaze faltered when it lit upon the bed—the very *large* bed—that occupied most of the small space.

Carol, or someone, had thoughtfully left Meg's suitcase and turned down the bed for them.

Meg took a couple of awkward steps backward, away from the bed, and right into Cole's arms. He took advantage of her proximity and dropped a soft kiss on her neck, but paused when she shivered. Damn, she was so obviously inexperienced. Mixed feelings roiled through him—was he doing the right thing?

He pulled back. Go slow, he reminded himself. She was new at this, and he wanted to make her first time a wonderful experience she'd always remember. "Are you sure you want to do this?"

"Yes," Meg breathed, then lurched when she moved to place her arms around his neck and grabbed on to him for balance.

Suspicion dawned in his mind. "Are you drunk?"

"No, of course not."

He held her away to give her a searching gaze, and she wobbled. Wonderful. "Then why are you swaying?"

"Because I'm not used to these heels, that's why."

"You didn't have any trouble before."

"Well, maybe the wine affected me a little, but I'm *not* drunk."

He crossed his arms and scowled at her. "Prove it."

"What?" She stood there, gaping at him as if he were crazy.

Cole could feel his ears turn red. All right, so maybe it was a little foolish, but he wasn't going to be responsible for seducing an intoxicated virgin, for heaven's sake. "Prove to me you're not drunk."

"You've got to be kidding."

"No, I'm not."

"*How?* Do you happen to have a portable Breathalyzer on you?"

Okay, he probably deserved the sarcasm, but he was determined to know. "Please, Meg, humor me."

She heaved a sigh. "All right. What do I do?"

"Stand up straight, close your eyes and stick both arms out parallel to the floor."

She did so. "Now what?"

"Now touch the tip of your nose with your right index finger."

She touched it, swaying only a little.

"Now your left."

She teetered again. Uncertain, Cole said, "Okay, now open your eyes and, placing one foot directly in front of the other, walk toward the door."

Meg tried to walk a straight line, but she wobbled so badly she couldn't do it. She gave him a defiant stare, but he only lifted one eyebrow.

He was right. She was drunk.

Fire lit in her eyes, and she reached down to slip the shoes off her feet. "Damn you, Cole McKenzie, see if *you* can walk with these damned things on!"

She flung the shoes at him. One missed, but the other caught him in the shoulder. A lucky throw...or had she aimed for it? "But—"

She advanced on him, eyes blazing. "Give me another one."

"What?"

"Give me another test," she enunciated clearly, as if he were the one whose senses were impaired.

He searched his mind frantically. "Uh, say your ABCs."

She did so, rapidly and with precision. "Now another one."

He squirmed. Was he wrong? "Um, count backward from twenty to ten."

Again, her response was rapid and accurate. "Am I drunk?" she demanded.

Now he really felt like a fool. A drunk wouldn't be able to even come close to doing that well. "Uh, no," he admitted. "You're not drunk."

"Good." She bent to gather up her discarded shoes. "Now, Officer, if I'm free to go..." She headed for the door.

Damn. Now he'd really blown it. "Meg, wait."

She kept moving, so he had no recourse but to place himself between her and the door and plead with her. "Please wait."

Her eyes blazed. "Why?"

Why? "Because...because...I just made an utter fool of myself."

"Granted. So?"

"So let me explain."

Her eyes narrowed. "Explain what?"

He breathed a sigh of relief. At least she'd stopped running and started talking. He reached out and caressed her cheek. Relieved when she didn't flinch away, he spoke in a soft tone. "Meg...I only wanted to make sure I'm not taking advantage of you."

The fires receded, and she gazed back at him with confusion in her eyes. "But I—I wanted it, too."

"I know, but since this is our first time together, I wanted to make sure nothing went wrong. Instead, I screwed everything up."

She averted her eyes, but didn't move her head under his caressing hand. He tilted her chin up. "Will you let me make it up to you—to make this a night to remember?"

Meg nodded, and Cole breathed a sigh of relief. He'd redeemed himself—or he would if he could only fulfill the promise he'd just made.

"Good," he said. "Let's start over, then." He turned off the light so that the only illumination in the room was provided by the three-quarter moon, and moved toward her in the darkened room. "Come here, sweetheart."

Meg came into his arms, and Cole bent to taste her lips. She seemed a little shy, but she melted pliably into his arms. Slow—go slow, McKenzie, he reminded himself. She might say she wanted excitement and thrills, but she was new at this and still might run like a frightened rabbit if he wasn't careful.

Her sweet, tentative kiss branded a trail of fire down his body. He'd never had a woman affect him so hard and so fast. She might be inexperienced, but she certainly was enthusiastic. Of course, she'd claimed to experience much of life vicariously through romance novels. What was in those books, anyway?

Her kiss deepened, and she moaned a sweet sigh of pleasure that was almost his undoing. They had barely even started, and already her breathing was as irregular as his.

He pulled back to stare down at her desire-swollen lips, her eyes half-lidded with anticipation. "Don't stop," she breathed.

He kissed her again, taking her head in both hands and giving her sensuous mouth the thorough attention it deserved, concentrating his whole attention on that one spot until she whimpered with pleasure.

Cole took her hands in his, then sat down on the foot of the bed and tugged her onto his lap. As he hugged her to him, he began wordlessly showing her just how she affected him.

Placing one hand around her waist to hold her in place, he used the other to tilt her head up to give her a soft, lingering kiss. She molded against him, and when he released her lips, she exhaled a sigh of pure pleasure and wound her arms around his neck.

Cole shifted his hold and kissed her behind one ear, nibbling his way inch by delicious inch down her neck until he was stopped by the fabric of her dress. Undaunted, he moved his mouth to the keyhole opening and kissed her there, then ran his tongue around the inside of the opening, grazing the top of her breasts.

Meg gasped, and he could see her breasts swell— those same soft mounds that had been tantalizing him all night as they swayed beneath the soft fabric of her dress.

Tightening his hold on her waist, Cole moved his mouth down to graze his teeth over one breast, and was rewarded by her indrawn breath. He glanced up, wanting reassurance that he wasn't going too fast, because he doubted he could go any slower.

She put one hand on either side of his face, then drew his head back down to her chest, showing him how much she enjoyed his attentions. Cole grinned to himself, then suckled one breast through the soft material and rolled the nipple of the other with his free hand. She gasped, but hung on tightly. When he pulled back for a moment, she made a small sound of distress.

"It's okay," he said, and gave her another lingering kiss on the mouth as he unfastened her collar. Not taking his eyes off hers, he peeled the fabric away from her shoulders and pulled the material down until it rested just above her nipples. He didn't want to scare her, and this gave her an out if she wanted one.

He gazed into her eyes, but saw nothing but acceptance, so he moved his head down to kiss the perfect valley between her breasts.

Meg moved then, shrugging out of the sleeves, grasping the top of the dress to tug it down and let it fall to her waist in one swift movement.

It was Cole's turn to inhale sharply as he gazed at her dusky pink-tipped breasts. "My God, you're beautiful." He filled his hands with them and ran his thumbs over the sensitive peaks.

Her breath quickened, urging him to bolder effort. He bent down to lave her breasts with his tongue, and his desire surged to an all-consuming passion.

She moved her hands to his chest and fumbled with the buttons there. "Let me touch you, too," she murmured.

Cole lifted his head, and seeing her eyes dark with desire, he unbuttoned his shirt and tossed it onto the floor. Meg ran her hands through the dark mat of hair on his chest, arousing him even more.

He moaned, then jerked in surprise when he felt her hand dip toward his waist. He urged her from his lap, then stood and finished pulling the dress off so that she stood before him wearing nothing but her virginal white underwear.

He bent down to kiss her calf, then ran his hands up the inside of her legs to make soft circles on her inner thighs, testing, teasing. Meg tensed, and he hesitated. She wasn't quite ready yet.

Slowing his pace, Cole kissed his way up her body, moving with barely controlled passion up over her hip and down into the curve of her waist. Climbing steadily over Meg's soft, trembling midriff, he continued his erotic journey until he finally reached her taut nipple.

She drew in a sudden breath, and Cole looked her in the eye. "Are you sure this is what you want?" he asked huskily. If it wasn't, they had better stop now, or he'd never be able to.

"I'm sure." With a look of excitement and trepidation, she reached down to place her hand against his straining trousers.

Her innocent touch was so unexpected that Cole groaned and closed his eyes, willing himself into submission. Meg must have taken that as encouragement, for she unclasped his belt buckle and tried to unzip his pants.

Her hands trembled so much that she botched the job, but Cole took the initiative and removed his shoes and socks, then tugged off his slacks. A moment later, his briefs were on the floor and Meg was gazing at him in openmouthed wonder.

He let her look her fill, wondering what she was thinking. Did he scare her? He wanted her to feel safe, comfortable—not terrified. As he watched, astonishment faded from her expression, to be replaced by rampant curiosity. With a look of intense interest, she reached out and wrapped her fingers around him and stroked.

Cole groaned and crushed her to him, his breathing ragged. Damn. He had to stop her before she set him off prematurely. "Wait," he said. "Wait."

Giving her a hot, deep, long kiss, he couldn't help but rub himself against her, stopping only when he heard her gasp.

Releasing her momentarily, he pulled her down so they could lie on the bed and slowed to run his hand down the erotic curve of her back to the elastic of her panties. Slowly he drew them off, until her entire body was exposed to his view.

Meg laid there, wide-eyed, staring at him, and he cupped her gently with his hand, trying not to frighten her. She gasped, and he worked his way up her body with his lips until he was once more suckling her breast. When she relaxed again, he dipped his finger inside her.

She was ready. More than ready. Her body was warm and welcoming, slick with her desire. He kissed her again. "You feel like silk. Hot silk."

She moved her hips against him, and he found her pleasure point and caressed it, exulting when small moans of delight escaped from her lips. Her gasps fueled his ardor until there was nothing in his consciousness except him, her, and the hot need between them. She opened her eyes momentarily to gaze at him, then tentatively reached down between them.

He forestalled her, saying, "No. Not now. Later. For now, just lie back and enjoy."

He continued to lavish attention on her sensitive breasts and the moist core between her legs, watching the progression of her desire in the way her breathing quickened and her hands clutched the sheets. He increased his ministrations, wanting her to experience the ultimate, then rejoiced when she finally cried out in pleasure and pulsed around him, throbbing against his hand.

Her complete abandonment to ecstasy made his own body's hunger more urgent. He had to have her—now. He kissed her hard and fast, then grabbed the condom from his shirt and donned it. Cradling her beneath him, he entered her, then paused.

She caressed his back and murmured, "It's okay."

Dear God, he hoped she meant it, because he couldn't stop now. He pushed through, then held his breath and stopped when she tensed. "Are you okay?"

"More than okay." She gave him a hard, deep kiss as she wrapped her legs around his waist.

Relieved beyond measure, he thrust into her all the way, barely registering her gasp of surprise. He paused for a moment to give her a questioning look, and Meg whispered, "More. I want more."

Cole's reservations fled. Slowly he stroked in and out, letting the sensations build and roll over him until he found himself pumping with a frenzy he couldn't control. Release came suddenly, and with it a transcendent feeling of joy he'd never before experienced. He convulsed once, twice, then collapsed to lie shaking in her arms.

He slowly regained his senses and glanced down at Meg, totally spent. He smiled and cradled her cheek in one hand, then gave her a gentle kiss. "Thank you," he whispered. "For the best experience of my life."

Meg smiled and caressed his cheek. "And thank *you* for making it so special."

Cole sighed in relief, then gathered her in a loving embrace. There, with Meg cradled in his arms, he fell fast asleep.

MEG WOKE shortly before dawn, and smiled down at Cole, sleeping beside her. They'd made love twice more during the night, each time Meg getting bolder and more exploratory, until she learned every plane and curve of his body. She hadn't known a man's body was so different from a woman's—in more than just the obvious places—and she was fascinated by the contrasts.

Carol was right. Meg had let Cole take her to bed, and now she was a goner. She wanted to be with this man always, but it couldn't be. Just contemplating it, she could see her dream slipping away. She couldn't have that—she couldn't let one little fling destroy everything she'd worked toward. Not now, not when she was so close.

Meg continued to watch Cole, silently thanking him for giving her this one night of passion. This one incredible night might have to last a lifetime if she lost the bet . . . or even if she won.

Because Cole was right, too. Even if she won the bet and moved to San Antonio, there was no guarantee her life would be any different. Just being in the big city might not be enough to make her happy.

She let her gaze drink its fill of the perfection of Cole's lean body until she heard a deep chuckle.

Cole grinned wickedly at her. "You look like you're trying to memorize me."

"I am. I want to remember you always like this."

He propped himself up on one elbow and smoothed her hair away from her face. "You act as though you'll never see me again after today."

Hadn't he been listening? "It's okay," she reassured him. "I don't expect anything."

He stilled in the act of caressing her arm and frowned. "You should. You're a very special lady, and you deserve the best."

That was a prelude to a brush-off if she'd ever heard one. A small pang pierced her chest, but she ignored it. She'd expected this, after all—and planned for it. It was the price she'd paid for a night of ecstasy. She placed her fingers against his mouth. "Shh."

His frown deepened, and he gathered her to him until they were lying full length against one another, skin to skin, sharing their warmth. He held her tightly. "We *will* see each other again. I'm moving to Lingston."

A mishmash of emotions swirled through her. Sharp pleasure, fear, disappointment. He was moving to Lingston, but in all likelihood, she'd be moving away.

She toyed with the idea of forgetting about Baby and staying in Lingston to be near Cole, but discarded it. It was best to let events run their course and win the bet, then move to the city. That way, they'd both have their dreams. If Cole was really serious about her, he'd look her up there.

Cole shook her slightly when she remained silent. "Meg? Did you hear me? I'm moving to Lingston. I want to see you again. Is that okay with you?"

"I may not be there. Why don't you stay in San Antonio? We can see each other there."

He shook his head. "No, I've decided. You've convinced me Lingston has a much better environment to raise my son, so I'm moving—his needs come first."

That was the trouble. They had conflicting needs . . . and dreams.

"Okay?" Cole persisted.

She kissed him and snuggled back down beside him. "Okay." *But I won't be there.*

BEAU PACED the small Phoenix hotel room in his underwear—his *dirty* underwear—muttering in annoyance. He wasn't sure he'd be able to get out of this situation with his bank account intact, so he'd sent the tuxedo off to be cleaned rather than buy a new set of clothes. If this didn't work out, he wouldn't have the wherewithal to buy a cup of coffee, let alone a pair of slacks.

He hated feeling grungy and dirty, and looking like a chump, but what choice did he have?

He grabbed the phone for at least the twentieth time and dialed Mr. Peterson's number, praying his boss would be at home this time. Ah, finally, an answer.

"Mr. Peterson?"

"Yes?"

"This is Beau. Beau Larrimer."

Mr. Peterson's voice turned cold. "Do you have the diamond?"

"Uh, not yet."

"You promised you'd have it back today."

"Yes, sir, I know. But—"

"No buts, Larrimer."

Beau interrupted before Peterson could fire him. "Wait, sir. I know where it is. Someone stole it from me, and I know how to get it back. I'll have it tomorrow, first thing."

When Peterson didn't say anything, Beau continued. "Please, give me a chance." He hated to beg, but he had no choice. He couldn't afford to pay for that ring. "It'll be in the store on Monday, I promise. If not, I'll pay for the diamond and you can fire me."

Peterson heaved a heavy sigh. "All right. One more chance. But if that ring's not back in the store on Monday—"

"It will be," Beau said, relief flooding through him. "It will be." Now all he had to do was find Natalie and convince her to give him back his ring.

Chapter Ten

Cole glanced at the clock by the bed and placed a kiss on Meg's shoulder. "We've got a couple hours until we have to meet the breeder, so..." He trailed off as Meg wiggled out of bed and headed toward the bathroom.

"Hey," he called, watching the bewitching swish of her derriere. "We don't have to leave right this minute."

Meg threw an easy grin over her shoulder. "That's okay. I want to have breakfast with Jim and Carol."

"What about me?" For the life of him, Cole couldn't help the plaintive note that crept into his voice.

She laughed. "You can have breakfast, too."

Cole watched in disbelief as she went into the bathroom and closed the door, then turned on the shower. What was going on here? Being her first lover, he'd been prepared for clinging or declarations of love. Hell, he wouldn't have been surprised to be on the receiving end of tears and recrimination, but... indifference? What kind of reaction was that?

He frowned and lay back on the bed, mentally reviewing his technique. Hadn't he done everything right?

First and foremost, he'd made sure that she was protected and that she enjoyed herself. And she *had* enjoyed herself, she'd even said so. She didn't seem to regret the loss of her virginity, either. Hell, she'd seemed to revel in it.

So had he, actually. Last night had been one of the most fantastic experiences of his life, and he really wanted to get to know this woman better. Much better. So, what was the matter with her?

A small internal voice reminded him that this was what he'd always said he wanted—great sex with no strings, no ties, no expectations.

So why did it annoy him so much when Meg said she didn't *expect* anything? He wasn't a love-'em-and-leave-'em kind of guy. At least he never had been before. Why did Meg automatically assume he was?

Well, hell, if that was what she wanted, that was what he'd give her, though he'd been looking forward to a couple more days of stolen kisses, heavy breathing and long, sensuous bouts of lovemaking. Instead, now he had to play it cool, too. Damn.

His annoyance didn't fade, not even in the face of Meg's irritating cheerfulness. He followed her into the main house for breakfast and scowled as she joked with Jim and Carol and the kids. She fit right in, as if she'd been born into the family—and Cole found himself the outsider.

He grumbled at everyone around him, but after giving him a couple of odd looks, they ignored him and let him eat his breakfast in brooding silence.

After that very unsatisfying breakfast, Cole and Meg left the little ones with Jim and Carol and headed for the breeder's place.

At least the meal had accomplished one thing—it had given him time to think. And he'd finally figured out the problem. Baby. It had to be that rabbit.

If Baby would just lose this contest thing, everything would be wonderful. Cole intended to move to Lingston to give his son the type of wholesome environment Luke needed. And if Meg lived there too, well, that was an added bonus he hadn't counted on.

Until now, he'd pretty much resigned himself to not finding another "significant other" until Luke was grown and gone. After all, how many women would want a ready-made family? And he hadn't expected there to be many prospects in a small town like Lingston.

But he might be wrong. If Meg was any indication, small-town life would be a hell of a lot more interesting than he'd expected. That was, if he could convince her to stay.

That was the problem. If Baby won the championship, then Pops would sell the farm and she'd leave Lingston like a shot. How could he convince her otherwise?

Silently, and a bit guiltily, Cole hoped the breeder refused to return Baby. It was the only way he could think of to keep Meg in Lingston.

They pulled up to Jackson Murphy's ranch house at the specified time, and a man came out to greet them. Cole's eyes widened—this guy was *huge*. He easily topped Cole by six inches and outweighed him by a good sixty pounds, with a scraggly beard and a mean expression that boded ill for Meg's dream.

Cole rejoiced at the sight of him. Murphy—if that was who it was—didn't look as though he'd relish giving back anything that belonged to him. Not even Meg would expect Cole to act like Rambo with this guy.

This was great. Cole would try as hard as he could to convince the guy to give them back the silly rabbit, and when that didn't work, Meg would at least know he'd tried his best. He felt a bit guilty about being so gleeful about it, especially since Meg would lose what she *thought* was her dream, but this was for the best, if only she'd realize it.

"Maybe you'd better let me handle this," Cole said.

Meg nodded, and they exited the car. He approached the big man, hand outstretched. "Murphy?"

"The same," the man said, and shook his hand. "What can I do for you?"

"We've come about the rabbit you purchased in El Paso."

Murphy frowned. "What about it?"

"Well, the man who sold it to you didn't own it. The rabbit actually belonged to Ms. Hollingsworth here." Cole nodded toward Meg.

"Hollingsworth? That's the name of the man who sold me the rabbit."

"I know—that's her brother. But he sold it without her knowledge or permission."

The big guy frowned again. "Why would he do that?"

Before Cole could say anything, Meg interjected. "It was a bet, you see."

His eyebrows rose. "What kind of bet?"

Meg explained it to him. Cole smiled as the farmer's scowl deepened. Good—the man would never agree now.

Murphy waited until Meg was done, then spoke. "You mean to tell me your brother and grandfather sold me the rabbit so you'd lose the bet by default?"

Meg nodded.

Murphy gave her a fierce frown. "That's dishonorable."

"Yes, it is," Meg agreed quietly.

It was Cole's turn to frown. Wait a minute. What had just happened here?

"Sure," Murphy said. "I'll sell you back your rabbit. Shoot, I'll *give* him back to you."

Meg smiled. "Oh, that won't be necessary. I'll return your check, and I already told my brother that if it cost us any more to get Baby back, he'd have to pay the difference."

The man laughed, a big hearty chuckle that rocked his massive frame. "Good for you. I think the price of the rabbit just doubled."

Meg laughed. "I thought it might."

"Come on," Murphy said. "Your rabbit is over here in this shed."

He led them to one of the outbuildings, and Cole followed. Damn. The giant had turned out to be a softy after all. Now Murphy and Meg were as thick as two thieves, and the best of buddies. Dejected, Cole followed them to the shed.

Inside the building, there were several rows of rabbits, all in wire mesh cages. He wrinkled his nose at the barnyard smell, but, truth to tell, it wasn't that bad. The area appeared well lit, well ventilated, and cleaner than he'd expected.

He glanced into one of the cages and snorted in disbelief. What ridiculous-looking animals. These Angora rabbits looked like giant white cotton puffs sitting on oversize feet, with a small pointed face sticking out the top. Even more absurd, they had little tufts of hair sticking out of their ears and feet like silly tassels.

Meg looked around in approval. "You keep a good place here."

"Thanks," Murphy said. "I keep the Angoras for my wife—she uses their fur to knit hats and sweaters as a side business." He walked over to a cage on the end. "We'd heard about Baby and wondered why you wanted to sell him when he was only one leg shy of winning grand champion status. Now we know."

"Why did you want him?" Meg asked.

"He has some good characteristics I need bred into my stock, so I'd planned to use him for stud."

What a great life. Just lie around all day, waiting for good-looking female rabbits to come to you? Baby had it made—if only he'd stay here.

"Well," Meg said. "You've been so nice about this that I'll make you a deal. If Baby wins tomorrow, I'll give him back to you. I'll have to sell all the rabbits, anyway, since I'll be moving to San Antonio."

"And if he doesn't win? Will you still sell him?"

Meg frowned in thought. "Maybe. But why don't you go ahead and use him for stud now, while we wait?"

Cole made a choking sound, and Meg turned to him. "Is that okay with you?"

"I guess so, but how long is it going to take?" He didn't want to hang around all day waiting for two bunnies to make love.

Meg and Murphy exchanged an amused glance. "Not long," Murphy assured him. "Not long at all. Watch."

He opened a cage farther down the row and grasped a rabbit by the ears, then supported it under its bottom and removed it from the cage.

"Is that Baby?"

"No. This is a doe. A female," Murphy replied. He carried the rabbit over to another hutch and opened the door. "This one is Baby."

Cole shrugged. They all looked alike to him. He gazed at the rabbit that had caused all this in the first place, singularly unimpressed. Why the fuss over such an ordinary-looking animal?

Murphy put the doe in the hutch with Baby, and Cole grimaced. Great, just what he wanted to do with his morning—sit around on his hands watching two rabbits make like bunnies.

Baby seemed to understand what the doe's presence meant, because he started jumping around the cage. If activity level was any indication, this was one excited rabbit.

The doe cowered in the corner at first, but Baby approached her and performed what Cole could only have described as bunny foreplay. He frantically rubbed his chin over the doe's back and hindquarters until she stopped trembling and raised her tail.

That must have been some kind of signal, for Baby reared up on his hind legs and had at her. A few seconds later, Baby emitted a stifled scream and fell from the female.

Cole gaped in astonishment. Maybe Baby was out of the running now. "What's wrong with him?"

Murphy gave him an odd look and reached in to draw out the doe. "Nothing's wrong with him. He's finished."

"You mean . . . that was it?"

"Sure." Murphy grinned. "Haven't you ever heard the phrase, 'quick like a bunny'?"

"Well, sure, but I never thought—" Cole shook his head. Damn. Here he'd thought Baby was down for the count, and it turned out he was only basking in the afterglow. He scowled at the satiated rabbit. Some stud.

Meg glanced at Cole in surprise. Just what did that strange expression mean? He looked almost . . . jealous. What was going through his mind?

Murphy took Baby out of the cage. "Your traveling box is over here." He carried the rabbit to the corner and put him inside with some food and water, then handed the box to Cole.

Putting Cole's strange mood out of her mind, Meg turned to the breeder and smiled, holding out her hand. "Thank you, Mr. Murphy. You've been very kind—and very understanding. I'll let you know about Baby later. Will you be coming to the fair in Phoenix?"

"Sure will. Hope we'll see you there." He grinned, and his eyes twinkled. "I'm anxious to see if you win your bet or not."

Meg gave him another smile, waved goodbye and followed a scowling Cole to the car.

When they got to the car, Cole frowned at the large box. "Where are we supposed to put this?"

"It'll fit in the back seat."

"This thing is huge. We won't have any room for the kids and the dog."

That was right—she'd momentarily forgotten about the rest of their entourage. She sighed. "Well, put it in the back seat for now. When we get to Jim and Carol's, we can transfer it to the trunk, and I can keep Baby in my lap for the rest of the trip. It's not all that far to Phoenix." Though how she was going to keep the kids and the dog away from Baby and his luxurious fur was a good question.

Cole placed the box in the back, and Meg entered the car, then gave the box a satisfied pat, her spirits high. Okay, now she had Baby back, and all she had to do was make it to Phoenix and enter him in tomorrow's judging. Finally, everything was going her way.

She smiled at Cole. "I wouldn't have been able to catch up to Jerry and discover where Baby was without you. Thanks for your help."

Cole gave her an odd look. "You're welcome," he muttered, and started the car. "So, what sort of chance does Baby have at winning this...thing?"

Meg waved farewell to Murphy as they drove away. "Pretty good. He's been judged best of breed, first in his class and best in show at two other fairs. The last two he got in the same show, so only one of them counts. If he can win one of them in Phoenix, then he automatically becomes a grand champion." She grinned at him. "And I win the bet."

"And you're still planning on moving to San Antonio?"

"You betcha," she said. Why would she stop then, when she was so close to getting exactly what she wanted?

Cole merely grunted, so Meg ignored him. Resolutely pushing memories of last night out of her mind, she went on to daydream about selling the farm and planning where to live in San Antonio. In no time, they were back at Jim and Carol's house.

They related their success and gathered up all their belongings, including the kids and the dog. As they prepared to leave, Carol gave Meg a big hug. "It was so nice meeting you. I hope I see you again some day."

Meg smiled. She really liked Cole's cousins. "Me too."

Carol grinned at Meg and whispered for her ears only. "Looks like you've caught yourself a McKenzie."

Meg pulled back to stare in disbelief. "You've got to be kidding."

"No," Carol said. "I've seen the way he looks at you. The man is smitten for sure, only I'm not sure he realizes it yet." She grinned. "I expect to hear any day now that we're going to be cousins-in-law."

Meg shook her head. "I don't know... If I win this bet, I probably won't ever see him again."

Carol gave her an odd look. "So, you'd rather win the bet, even if it means you'll never see Cole again?"

She'd been avoiding that. "I don't know...."

Carol chuckled. "Well, I hope you figure it out before it's too late." She gave her husband a fond look. "But I've never regretted marrying my McKenzie."

Jim shouted over to them, "Hey, you two, quit gabbing. Cole and Meg need to get on the road."

Meg nodded and gave Carol one last hug. "Thanks for everything. You've given me a lot to think about, and I promise I won't make a rash decision."

They somehow managed to get the kids strapped in the back seat with the dog, and settled the rabbit in front with Meg. Jim stuck his head in the open window on Cole's side and grinned. "So have you got everyone? Want a few more?"

Cole looked around at the full car. "I think we have more than our share, thank you." He stuck out his hand and shook Jim's. "Thanks again for taking care of them for us."

"No problem." Jim stepped back away from the car as Cole started the ignition.

They pulled out of the driveway, and Jim and Carol waved goodbye. As Meg watched, Jim placed an arm around his wife's waist and gave her an affectionate kiss while their kids hugged their legs.

Now *that* was what a family was supposed to be—not the sterile environment she'd grown up in. Unfortunately, Pops was uncomfortable with affection and had always admonished her to be sensible. There was no place for impulse or whimsy in her home.

She stared after the McKenzies wistfully, then shook her head and brought herself back down to earth. No sense in wishing for what she could never have—Pops and Jerry just weren't the homey type. Instead, she'd be better off sticking to her original plan and trying to build a better life for herself.

As they headed out of town, Cole was strangely quiet, though the kids and dog more than made up for it. Luckily, Lady hadn't discovered the rabbit in Meg's lap, so the dog was content to lie in the back and let the children play with her.

Once the kids settled down a little, Meg's attention drifted once more to Cole, and, inevitably, to the desire they'd shared last night. She felt her cheeks flush as she recalled the pleasure she'd felt in his arms. Yes, it was worth it. Even if she never felt such delight ever again, she was glad to have had this one night with him.

Susie broke into her thoughts. "Aunt Meg, I gotta go potty."

Meg exchanged an amused look with Cole and sighed. "I really had hoped to make it all the way to Phoenix without seeing another public rest room."

Cole chuckled. "Looks like you're out of luck." He glanced back at Susie. "There's one coming up pretty soon."

He pulled up to a rest stop, and Meg got out of the car one more time to help the children into the bathroom. As she waited for them to finish, she heard a strange sound and glanced around the room, spotting a small ball of white fur in the corner—a cat.

The pitiful thing gazed up at her and gave her a plaintive little meow that tugged at her heartstrings. "Oh, you poor thing." She reached down to pick the cat up, and it rubbed its face against hers and purred.

The kids came racing up and peered up at her. "Whatcha got?" Susie asked.

"A kitty. See?"

"Me see," Luke said in an imperative tone of voice, and strained on tiptoe to see the animal.

Meg leaned down to give him a better look, and before she could stop him, he darted one hand out to pat the cat on the head.

The cat shrank back against Meg, its ears flat, and hissed at the little boy. Luke's eyes grew round and he backed off.

"It's okay, Luke," Meg reassured him. "He's just a little scared right now. You need to move slow and easy, so he knows you're not going to hurt him."

Luke nodded, his eyes wide, but didn't come any closer.

Susie piped up. "Are you gonna keep him?"

Meg nodded. "The poor guy appears to be abandoned, just like Lady. We can't leave him here, can we?"

Susie and Luke shook their heads and followed Meg out of the bathroom to the car.

Cole took one look at her and froze, then shook his head. "No. Absolutely not. You are *not* adding a cat to this circus."

Meg gave him a pleading look, but didn't expect much. He'd already been more than understanding when he'd added Susie and the puppy as well as Luke to their crazy cross-country trip. "He's lost and scared," she said.

Cole groaned, rolling his eyes. "Just how do you expect to keep the dog, the cat *and* the rabbit apart in the car?"

Meg grinned. He didn't know it yet, but he'd already capitulated. "I'll think of something. Please, Cole?"

He just shook his head. "You're one crazy lady, you know that?"

Even the kids knew that meant yes, so they laughed and jumped up and down. "Oh, boy," Susie said. "A kitty." Susie apparently felt this animal was her own special pet, since the rabbit was Meg's and Luke seemed to have appropriated the dog.

"All right, everyone," Cole said, "back in the car."

Meg held on to the cat until Cole had strapped the children in and settled the puppy on the floorboard under Luke's feet. Baby was in the front seat, so...where should she put the cat? Cats liked high places, so maybe it would be best to put him up in the rear window, so he'd be safe from the dog *and* the children.

Meg placed the cat up in the window and was satisfied when he stayed there. He didn't seem too happy with his new position, but she figured he'd soon learn the wisdom of it. Satisfied, she got into her seat and placed Baby in her lap.

Cole shook his head and rolled down his window. "It's getting a little crowded in here with these rest-stop rejects. What's next? An alligator?"

As he put the car in gear and backed out of the parking spot, Meg couldn't resist teasing him a little. "Don't be silly. No one abandons an alligator at a rest stop." She paused, considering. "Not in Arizona, anyway."

Cole laughed. "But if they did, you'd rescue him, wouldn't you?"

Meg pretended to think about it. "Maybe...but I doubt he'd fit in the car."

"Thank heaven for small favors."

Cole's chuckle was cut off when a loud hiss came from the back seat. Meg whirled around to see Susie out of her seat belt and lunging for the cat. Cole hit the brakes, and the cat leaped down on the seat to get away, still hissing.

Luke grabbed for him and missed. Lady, spotting this new potential playmate, jumped up to place her front paws on the seat. She barked once, and the cat yowled. His eyes darted back and forth and, seeing no escape from the terrors of the back seat, he leaped to the front.

Meg shoved him aside, away from Baby's precious fur, and the hapless cat ended up on Cole's shoulder.

It was hard to say who was more surprised or upset about their sudden union—Cole or the cat.

"Yow!" Cole and the cat howled simultaneously.

Meg winced in sympathy. The cat had all four sets of claws firmly embedded in Cole's shoulder.

Cole snatched the cat by the scruff of the neck and yanked him off. He tried to drop him between the seats, but the cat wasn't having it. He snarled, then raked his claws across Cole's unprotected forearm. Cole wisely let go, and the cat spotted freedom in the form of the open window. Frantically he scrambled up and over Cole and leaped out of the car.

Meg sighed in relief, but couldn't help giggling when she saw the shock on Cole's face. He looked as though he'd just been hit by a tornado with fangs and didn't quite know what to do about it.

"Well," Meg said, in an exaggerated tone of disgust, "aren't you going after him?"

Cole turned to stare at her in disbelief, and she burst out laughing. The look of relief that immediately followed, when he realized she was kidding, was even more comical and she laughed harder.

"I'm so glad you find my pain amusing," Cole said with a quirk of his eyebrow.

"Poor baby," Meg crooned, but the effect was spoiled by her giggling. "There's a first aid kit in the trunk. Why don't we park the car and I'll take care of your battle wounds?"

Cole gave her an enigmatic look, but did as she suggested. "Very funny."

He turned around to stare at the children, who were sitting stock-still in their seats. Susie had wisely refastened her belt and was staring at him, wide-eyed. After chastising her for not remaining in her seat belt, he said, "We're only going to be out of the car for a minute or two. Don't move—either of you. Got it?"

They nodded, clearly impressed at the stern look on Cole's face. Even the puppy appeared suitably chastened, so Cole and Meg both exited the car.

After seeing what happened with the cat, Meg wasn't about to let those three back seat monsters anywhere near Baby, so she placed him temporarily in his cage for safekeeping.

Cole went back into the rest room to wash his scratches, and she pulled out the first aid kit to find the necessary supplies to treat his wounds. When he came back out, she unfolded a premoistened alcohol pad and dabbed at the scratches on his arm.

"Ow, that stings."

Meg grinned. Men were such babies sometimes. She stopped, pad held poised above his forearm. "If you'd rather do this yourself..."

He grimaced. "No—just get it over with quick, okay?"

Meg tried not to smile as he winced when she applied the alcohol. Wickedly, she hummed the tune to "Cat Scratch Fever," but broke off laughing when Cole gave her a dirty look. "All right," she said. "Now your shoulder."

"My shoulder?"

"It was clawed, too, wasn't it?"

Cole flexed his shoulder. "Yeah."

"Okay, then, take off the shirt."

He did as she asked, and Meg had him sit down on the bumper while she surveyed the damage. The cat had certainly done a number on him. Long, bloody gashes crossed his right forearm, and his back looked almost as bad. Two long sets of parallel scratches slashed across the back of his right shoulder. Meg dabbed the alcohol against his skin, and Cole winced, pulling away from her slightly.

"Oh, don't be such a big baby," she said.

"Well, if you'd warn a guy..."

"You want to get better, don't you?"

He slanted a grin up at her. "Can't you just kiss it better?"

Her heart stopped for a moment as she gazed into his brown eyes and remembered all the places where she'd kissed him last night. She averted her gaze. "I'm sorry," she said in a deliberately light tone, "but that's not the recommended prescription in this situation."

His grin widened and his voice turned husky. "Oh, what is?"

She waved a white tube at him. "Antibiotic ointment. That's what you need."

Cole's mouth twisted in a half smile. "Oh. Well, what I had in mind would sure be a lot more fun."

Meg's heart beat faster as she applied the ointment. Undoubtedly, he was right. But she couldn't think about that now, and she certainly didn't need the distraction.

"What about the front?" Cole asked.

"Huh?"

"The front," he repeated. "The cat got me here, too." He turned around, and she could see that the cat had gouged him right beneath the collarbone. She glanced down and sucked in her breath.

Damn. That was a mistake. Cole was just too damned good-looking for his own good. With that sexy go-to-hell grin, tight jeans and hard-muscled chest, with its mat of dark curls, he could give that guy in the diet Coke commercial a run for his money any day.

She hesitated, and Cole grinned again. "What's the matter, Meg? Cat got your tongue?"

Meg shook herself out of her reverie and chuckled. "No, but it sure looks like he had you for lunch." Swiftly she swabbed the pad across Cole's scratches, and was rewarded by a sharp indrawn hiss.

Unfortunately, his chest muscles flexed at the same time, and Meg couldn't help but remember the feel of his chest beneath her eager fingers, his mouth against hers, and his—

"Meg?"

She blushed, embarrassed to be caught daydreaming about his body. Quickly she made herself focus on just the one part that needed attention.

And just which part is that, Meg?

No, damn it, don't think about *that*. The scratch. Yes, that's it. The scratch. Swiftly she applied the ointment to his injury, slapped a bandage over it and stepped back with a sigh of relief. "There. All better."

Cole grinned as he shrugged his shirt back on. "Not quite. You still haven't kissed it."

A tender longing built within her, so deep and poignant that she positively ached. The feelings she'd been suppressing all morning surged forth to smother her. This man—this sexy, funny, caring man—had not only indulged her silly whim with the cat, he hadn't even reproached her when he was torn up as a result.

She bit her lip and stared at him. He was dark and dangerous, all right. Dangerous to her sanity, dangerous to her dreams...dangerous to her heart.

Realization struck, and Meg involuntarily stepped back and put a hand over her heart. She loved him. It had only been two days, but she'd fallen in love with him.

No—it wasn't supposed to happen like this. Her first love was supposed to be ecstatic, world-shattering.

Well, world-shattering it was, but not ecstatic. Instead, all she felt was a great sadness. He was just supposed to be a one-night stand. She *couldn't* fall in love with Cole—not a man who wanted to settle down in the back of beyond and raise kids and chickens, for heaven's sake. Damn it, why couldn't he stay in San Antonio?

Cole interrupted her reverie once again. "Meg? Are you all right?"

"I—I'm okay," she lied.

BEAU PACED the Phoenix hotel room yet again. He'd searched the whole fair, but hadn't found hide or hair of Natalie or Cole...or that damned rabbit.

They were bringing the rabbit in for judging, so he'd just have to continue watching until they showed up. He had no choice. There was only one day left to get the ring. If he didn't return it by tomorrow, he was dead meat.

Chapter Eleven

As they pulled up to the Arizona State Fairgrounds, Cole heaved a sigh of relief. The trip from Tucson to Phoenix wasn't long, but it had sure seemed that way after trying to keep the kids and animals apart. Thank heavens the cat had had the sense to get the heck out of this madhouse. Lord only knew what would've happened if he'd stuck around, too.

And what was the matter with Meg? Cole thought he'd seen an echo of passion in her eyes when she nursed his scratches, but she'd spent the rest of the trip avoiding his gaze and tending the menagerie.

Did she regret their lovemaking? He hoped not—he definitely wanted a repeat performance, but more than that, he wanted to convince her to stay in Lingston so he could get to know her better. For now, though, they had to take care of that damned rabbit.

He parked the car, then he and Meg gathered the kids, the dog and the rabbit together and headed off to the livestock barn. Meg got Baby squared away for the competition the next day, then heaved a big sigh.

Cole glanced at her. "What's that for?"

She gave him a halfhearted laugh. "I guess until this moment I wasn't sure we'd even make it this far. I was afraid something would happen to Baby, or that Beau would pop up somewhere and claim the rabbit had swallowed his diamond or something."

Cole chuckled and slung an arm about her shoulders. "Well, Beau's undoubtedly found his ring by now, so you have nothing to worry about there. Now all you have to do is wait for the outcome of the judging."

Meg nodded, but stiffened when he tried to hug her. Cole awkwardly removed his arm from her shoulder, feeling as if he'd just sprouted a new appendage and didn't know what to do with it. What was wrong? Was she remembering how much was riding on this—or was it *him* she had problems with?

Luckily, a woman hurried up to distract them. "Meg Hollingsworth?"

Meg nodded.

"I've got a note for you." The woman handed over a folded piece of paper.

Meg murmured her thanks and scanned the note. "Hmm... Looks like Pops flew here to see the outcome of the judging. He wants us to meet him at his hotel."

Cole raised an eyebrow. "You want to go or not?"

"Sure," she said with a grimace. "I want to give the old reprobate a piece of my mind."

When they got to the hotel, Meg's grandfather and brother were waiting there, along with Natalie. After Meg introduced Cole and left the children playing quietly in the corner, the skinny little old man gazed at her with contrition in his eyes. "I'm sorry, Meggie."

She glared at him. "You should be. What would Gram say if she were alive?"

The old man hung his head, but didn't answer.

Meg's glare abated, to be replaced by concern. "You don't look so good. Have you taken your medicine today?"

Pops's expression was guilty. "No, I...forgot, what with the trip and everything."

"Did you at least remember to bring it with you?"

Pops nodded. "I think it's in my shaving kit."

"Then go and get it."

Natalie rose. "Never mind. I'll get it." She fetched the pills from the other room and fussed around Meg's grandfather until he took them. "If I'd known about your medication, I would've made sure you took it. You can't take any chances with your health, you know."

Cole's eyebrows rose. This was a side of Natalie he'd never seen before. Then again, Cole and Luke were fairly self-sufficient and didn't care much for coddling.

Meg looked almost as surprised as he felt, but she took Natalie's change of attitude in stride and detailed the rest of her grandfather's health problems. Natalie listened with an intent expression, and Cole glanced over to catch a sly, satisfied smile on Pops's face.

Why, the old goat. He just wanted someone around to fuss over him, and it seemed he preferred that someone to be female. Cole would have laid odds the old man's health wasn't as bad as he made it out to be. What if Meg did leave to go off on her own? Would Pops really wither and die, as she seemed to expect, or would he be able to take care of himself? Cole suspected the latter, so he decided to keep an eye on the old fraud.

The old man started to relax, but Meg finished her litany of problems and turned to him again. "You're not off the hook, you know. No thanks to you, Baby is finally entered in the competition. Our bet is still on, right?"

Her grandfather nodded.

Meg cocked her head and narrowed her eyes. "Can I trust you to keep to the terms?"

Pops managed to look wounded. "Of course, Meggie. But *you* remember," he said, defiance rising in his voice, "if Baby doesn't win, you have to stay in Lingston and never talk about moving again."

Before Meg could answer, Jerry rose to stand next to the old man and pat him on the shoulder. "She remembers, Pops. We're real sorry, Meg—we didn't realize how much this meant to you. We'd like to make it up to you. What can we do?"

Cole smiled. "You could take the kids and the dog around the fair while I take Meg."

Natalie and the two men glanced at each other, and then Jerry nodded. "Sure. If that's what Meg wants."

She hesitated, then said, "Sure."

"Okay," Cole said. "We'll pick them up tomorrow at the judging."

They kissed the kids goodbye and left. Meg glanced up at him. "Thanks."

"For what?"

"Getting them to agree to let me go out on my own without a fuss."

He shrugged. "Jerry offered. I just took him up on it."

"Whatever—I'm just glad it worked."

"Good. Now we can have fun without worrying about the kids or the dog—or visiting every bathroom at the fair." Cole tried putting his arm around her shoulders again.

She stiffened, then relaxed. "Fun . . . yeah, that's a good idea. Let's have some fun. After all, this may be the last time we see each other."

Last time? Not if he could help it. He wouldn't tell her that, though—not if believing that was what helped her accept his arm around her. Instead, he resolved to show her a terrific time and give her a day to remember—even if Baby didn't win. And damned if he wouldn't give her something to remember Cole McKenzie by, too.

They spent the rest of the day exploring every inch of the fairgrounds, playing all the games, riding all the rides and eating almost everything in sight. After being jaundiced by the sights and sounds of the big city, Cole hadn't believed he could take such pleasure in this kind of entertainment, but he'd surprised himself and enjoyed it all right along with her as they ignored all their cares and set out just to have fun.

Most of all, he savored the sound of her laughter and the enchantment in her eyes. She took such delight in little things, indulging all her senses at once with the sweet taste of cotton candy, the smell of popcorn, the sound of children's squealing laughter, the brightly painted rides and the heart-jolting thrill of the roller coaster.

Once night fell, the carnival took on a different, less manic atmosphere. The mood turned slower, more romantic, as the children went home and couples roamed the fair arm in arm.

Cole grinned at Meg as they strolled down the midway, arms about each other's waist. Her other arm was full of the prizes they had won, and she was busy trying to stuff a funnel cake into her mouth. She looked tired, but happy.

An overwhelming feeling of tenderness washed over him. She was so sweet, so whimsical, so special, so...so...Meg that he couldn't help but stare at her. What was it about her that made him feel this way?

Realization suddenly blindsided him. He loved her.

It hit him so hard, all he could do was stop and stare, openmouthed. Yes, he loved her. This was the woman he wanted to spend the rest of his life with, raising children, puppies, rabbits...whatever. He didn't care, so long as he had her by his side.

"What?" Meg asked, staring at him in concern. "Do I have sugar all over my face?"

Cole shook himself out of his reverie, trying to regain his cool and wondering whether the shock showed on his face. "Oh, a little." He brushed at her cheek to remove some of the sticky stuff and cast about for something to say. "Uh, why don't we ride the Ferris wheel? It's the only ride we haven't tried."

Meg wrinkled her nose. "It's a little tame, isn't it?"

"Yes, but I could use tame right now. I almost lost my dinner on that last one."

Meg laughed up at him. "Some tough guy you are."

He needed the distraction. "Please?" he asked, and tried to look pitiful.

"Oh, all right. If you insist."

Cole settled them in the Ferris wheel, moving the prizes to one side so he could put his arm around her. He wanted Meg all to himself, so that he could explore this new feeling in private. "So, are you having fun?"

Meg sighed happily. "Yes. Very much. I wish this day would never end." She laid her head on his shoulder and gazed up at the clear night sky as the Ferris wheel soared high into the air, rocking them with a gentle motion.

Cole's arm tightened around her. He knew the feeling. He, too, wished this day would never end—especially since tomorrow would bring with it Baby's judging and Meg's final decision.

After seeing her so happy today, he didn't know which he wanted more—for Baby to win or lose. If Baby won, he might never see her again, but if she lost, she'd lose all chances of fulfilling her dream.

Though he couldn't sympathize with her dream, he knew what it was like to have one. He would do almost anything to achieve his dream for Luke. So how could he deny Meg hers?

He couldn't. He gave Meg a sad smile and resolved to do whatever he had to help make her dream come true—even if it meant he'd never see her again.

Their car swayed as the ride came to a stop to let off some passengers. She yawned, her eyes half-shut.

Cole let his lips brush her hair. "Hey, sleepyhead, do you think you can stay awake long enough to get off this ride?"

Meg nodded into his shoulder. "Mmm-hmm..." She snuggled even closer, and Cole felt another wave of emotion wash over him—the instinctive urge to protect, to comfort, to cherish. He held her close, wanting to make every moment of their time together count. The ride came to a stop all too soon, and Cole helped her out, asking, "Are you through for the day?"

"Nope. I want to savor every moment, ride every ride."

Cole chuckled. "You've already ridden every ride. Some of them two or three times."

She frowned like a little girl denied a treat. "But I don't want this day to end."

He kissed her on the forehead, gently, so as not to startle her. "It doesn't have to."

The question on her face segued into a devilish twinkle. "One last fling?"

Disappointment stabbed through him. Was that how she saw him? As one more check mark on Meg's List of Exciting Things to Do? He glanced down into her eyes, and his annoyance evaporated. If she thought that, then she was fooling herself. She wanted him, all right—he could tell by her flushed cheeks and the longing in her eyes.

But what did she want him *for?* For just one more night? Or could he persuade her that she couldn't live without him? He didn't know, but he was sure going to try to convince her of the latter.

"Sure," he said. "One last fling."

MEG SHIVERED with excitement as Cole drove her to a nearby hotel—far away from where Pops and Jerry were staying. One more night with Cole wouldn't hurt, she assured herself. After all, her heart wasn't in any further danger—she'd lost it to him already.

She knew she was right when they entered the room and Cole gathered her in his arms, just where she'd longed to be all day. He released her, only to cradle her head in his hands and kiss her, softly at first, then deeper, more demanding. Her heart beat in her chest like a wild thing. Now this…this was what she'd been waiting for.

When he pulled back for a moment, she sighed with pleasure. "More…"

He tried to remove his hands, but she felt them stick to her face, caught in the sticky residue of the cotton candy and powdered sugar. He peeled his fingers away and chuckled, licking her chin. "I knew you were sweet, but…"

Chagrined, Meg tried to brush some of the sugar off. "Oh, Lord, I'm filthy. Maybe I should take a shower first?"

Cole grinned and hugged her to him, trailing kisses down her neck. "Good idea. We'll take one together."

Meg froze. "Together? I— You mean—?" Her pulse accelerated.

"Um-hmm..." he murmured as he tugged her blouse from her jeans and pulled it over her head. "Lots more fun that way."

"Oh." Her breathing quickened. She didn't know what he intended, but this was definitely what she'd had in mind when she set out to find excitement a few days ago.

She put up no resistance when Cole peeled off the rest of her clothing. He stood looking at her, murmuring, "You're so beautiful."

His simple words created a stab of sharp elation in her chest, and she wound her arms around his neck for another kiss.

Cole ran his hands down her back to cup her buttocks in both hands. She gasped in surprise at the sudden erotic pleasure that rocketed straight to the center of her being. It pooled there, then spread in circles of bliss throughout her body.

Cole opened his eyes to give her a questioning glance. More...she wanted more. She wanted to see all of him, feel all of him...against her, inside her, whatever it took. Quickly, with shaking hands, she divested him of his clothing until they stood naked flesh against naked flesh.

Cole grasped one breast in his hand and bent to lavish attention on it with his tongue. Before she could get caught up in the seductive sensations, Meg stopped him. "Wait. You promised me a shower."

He chuckled deep in his chest. "So I did."

He gave her breast one final nuzzle, then waited while she grabbed a condom from her suitcase. Capturing her hand in his, he pulled her into the bathroom and into the shower, where he grabbed a bar of soap, then turned the water on, hot and steamy, and steered her against the shower wall.

She gasped as her back hit the cold tile, but it was warmed in a moment as he braced himself on either side of her and kissed her thoroughly. As she returned his kiss with interest, the water beat down on them, producing a thick, heavy mist that made their desire seem almost tangible.

He rubbed himself against her, his erection as hard as a rock and twice as solid. She stroked the hard column of his flesh, exulting when he closed his eyes and moaned softly. Loving the way her touch seemed to excite him all the more, she cupped him with her other hand and increased her ministrations until his breathing turned ragged.

"No, wait," he gasped out, and stilled her hands. "Not yet."

"Why not?" she asked, pressing a lingering kiss against his neck and running her hands through the hair on his chest.

"I can't think when you do that," he murmured. "Besides, you're not clean yet."

He leaned away from her to unwrap the soap, and she released him, drinking in the sheer beauty of his lean, hard body. Water poured over his head and shoulders, running down his chest to make rivulets in the dark mat of hair and part around the full evidence of his desire.

Finding it hard to keep herself from touching him, Meg stood there against the damp shower wall, naked, her breasts heaving and her breath coming fast between her parted lips. She wondered what he had in mind as he gazed at her meaningfully and rubbed the soap between his palms.

From the look on his face, he had plans for that soap. Special plans.

He raised it with exquisite slowness, and her gaze followed like a magnet as he glided the slick bar over her shoulder. She released her breath in a sigh. That felt good—smooth and warm. Meg licked her lips and watched as Cole ran the soap down both her arms to gently wash each finger, then up again to cleanse her neck and face.

It was the most tender, most erotic thing she'd ever experienced. He'd hardly touched her, yet he'd made love to her with that bar of soap just as surely as if he'd entered her.

Cole pulled back again and held her gaze with his, steam rising around them to veil his intent expression. She watched, mesmerized, as he soaped his hands again, then ran them from her neck down to her breasts. He paused there, kneading them lightly.

Her breathing grew heavier. Dear God, this was heaven. His hands were warm, slick, infinitely pleasurable. Meg moaned and closed her eyes, then grabbed his shoulders, wordlessly begging for more.

Cole gave it to her, rolling her nipples between his fingers until they stood at attention. Once she thought she could bear it no longer, he allowed his hand to drift lower, down over her abdomen, to the nest of curls between her legs.

As he toyed with her breast and let his other hand drift lower, he asked, "Are you sore?"

"Only a little." Certainly not enough to make him stop.

Cole gave her an enigmatic smile and released her to retrieve the soap again. He leaned down to stroke it over her knee, then up her thigh, and finished nestled between her legs.

Meg inhaled sharply, but grabbed him with both hands and held on tight as he kissed her abdomen and worked the soap into a lather between her legs. He took her to a new plateau of sensation—dizzying sensation, where nothing existed but Cole, her, and the delicious friction of their bodies rubbing together. She didn't want to ever let go, because this felt so good, so right.

Later, much later, he set the soap aside. "Feel better?"

She was beyond words, and could only answer with a whimper. Cole rose to kiss her again, then slipped his finger inside her.

Meg arched against his hand as Cole found her pleasure point, and rained kisses on her face while he kneaded her breast with his other hand. The universe narrowed to two pulsating points of sensation, shaped and given form by the clever hands of Cole McKenzie, until there was nothing left but sheer feeling.

The tension mounted and suddenly released, giving way to pure carnal bliss that made her star go nova and pulse with the sudden release. She came back to earth slowly and felt herself throb against his hand.

Wanting to give him the same joy he'd just given her, she picked up the small package she'd brought with her into the shower. Unwrapping it with shaking fingers, she gave Cole a questioning look.

He glanced down at the condom in her hand and then stared back at her, his gaze smoldering, his body tight with tension. His message was clear. He wanted her to put it on.

She smiled and prolonged the moment, caressing him, teasing him. Then, when she sensed he was almost at his limit, she slowly unrolled the condom down his full length.

He inhaled sharply, then rose and entered her swiftly, filling her completely as he drove her inexorably against the shower wall.

She gasped. It felt so good, so right. Cole paused for a moment to give her a questioning look, and Meg adored him then. Even though he was practically trembling with desire and the need to move within her, he was still concerned about her feelings, *her* needs and desires.

"I'm okay," she reassured him.

Cole expelled a sigh of relief, then slowly pulled away and thrust in again. Meg's eyes widened, and her arms tightened around him as she raised one leg to wrap around his waist.

He grinned then, a wicked affirmation of his desire, and began to move in and out in long, slow strokes that feathered sweet curls of pleasure up and down her body. She let herself go in the sensation, riding the waves with him, shooting the curl and coming gasping out of the deep valley between swells.

The waves came harder, faster, until a veritable tsunami rocked her and spilled her back into the real world. Simultaneously, Cole emitted a feral cry and froze, poised above her with an indescribable expression.

Meg slid her leg down his and paused for a few moments to regain her equilibrium. "Cole?"

The water poured over him as he kissed her shoulder and held on tight. "Yes?" He grated the one word out.

"I'm clean now."

He laughed into her shoulder. "Inside and out."

She chuckled along with him, then kissed him—a long, lingering, deep kiss.

"But we're not done yet," he whispered. "Not by a long shot. I'm going to give you a night you'll never forget."

BEAU LURKED around the rabbit pens early in the morning, waiting for Natty to show up. He felt a little conspicuous in the remnants of his tuxedo, though he'd rolled up the shirtsleeves and removed the cummerbund. The problem was, he didn't look like the average fairgoer, and the locals were starting to eye him warily. Damn. Where was Natty?

Speak of the devil . . . there she was. Now all he needed to do was take her aside, explain about the ring in his most charming manner and convince her to give it back to him.

He smoothed back his hair, prepared to approach her, when he saw a man lean close and whisper something in her ear. Beau froze. Did Natty have a new boyfriend already?

No, it was that guy Jerry, the thief. Beau ducked into a corner and peered out at them. Natty batted her eyelashes and played up to the hayseed for all she was worth—and the old coot with him, too. What was the matter with her, anyway? Had she lost all sense of judgment?

There was no reason to suck up to hicks like this, when she could have Beau, unless . . . she had the diamond and knew Beau was coming after her. Sure, that was it. She was surrounding herself with infatuated men so Beau couldn't get to her.

That made a heck of a lot more sense than preferring these farmers to him. The only thing that surprised Beau was that she didn't have her cop ex-husband hanging around, too. Beau glanced around. Or was he?

That guy sure knew how to put a damper on things, and this would be a whole lot riskier if he was around. Well, better safe than sorry. Beau would just play it by ear until he could get Natty alone to talk to her. And this time, he wouldn't be quite so nice.

Some of the locals started giving him peculiar looks again, so he grabbed a straw cowboy hat off a nearby nail and shoved it on his head, then picked up a broom and tried to appear busy.

A half hour later, Beau realized she wasn't going to be alone for the foreseeable future. He had pushed the same dirt around the floor long enough. If something didn't happen soon, he was going to go nuts.

Something did. Natalie's kid . . . Matthew? Mark? No, Luke, that was it. Luke wandered away from his mother while she was making goo-goo eyes at the hayseed.

This could be Beau's chance—maybe he could persuade the boy to tell him where the ring was, so that he didn't have to worry about Natty at all. Beau followed Luke to the other aisle out of sight of his mother and leaned down to smile at the kid. Luke gave him a doubtful look, so Beau searched his mind for something kids liked. Dogs—this kid liked dogs. "Want to see some puppies?" he whispered.

The kid glared at him. "Me have puppy."

Beau kept his voice low. "Sure you do, but I know where there are lots of puppies. Cute, cuddly puppies who want little boys to play with."

Luke's eyes lit up, but he glanced over toward his mother.

To sidetrack him, Beau straightened and feigned nonchalance, saying, "Oh, never mind. I can see you're not interested. You're probably too noisy, anyway."

He started to walk away in the opposite direction from Natty and, just as he'd hoped, Luke followed.

The kid tugged on his pant leg, and Beau pretended annoyance as he stopped to hear what the boy had to say.

"*Not* noisy," he declared in a loud stage whisper.

Beau shrugged. "Okay, come along then." Inside, he rejoiced. Finally, the ring was within his grasp.

SADNESS washed over Meg as she snuggled up to Cole's warmth. There was no doubt about it—she was in love with him, and there was nothing she could do about it.

Unfortunately, the qualities that had made her fall in love with him were the very things that made it so impossible to continue this relationship. He was kind, and gentle, and cared a great deal about other people.

Why had she had to fall in love with such a nice man, anyway? Nice wouldn't cut it in the type of life she envisioned for herself. Nice was too safe, too seductive, too predictable. Nice would get her married, barefoot and pregnant in no time at all, and doom her to a boring existence forever.

Or at least that was the part of Cole she'd seen yesterday afternoon. Then there was the part of his personality that seemed to want to take over where Pops and Jerry left off. She didn't need that either. What she needed was a nice compromise—preferably one who lived in San Antonio.

Cole woke then and gave her a lazy smile, reaching out to capture her hand in his. "Good morning."

Her heart turned over, and she almost threw caution overboard and said to hell with it. This man was so incredibly handsome and sweet and sexy—how could she live without him?

Gram's voice intruded once again. "You have to follow your dreams, child. Always follow your dreams." Gram was right. If Meg didn't, she'd always regret it.

"Good morning," she responded, but pulled away. She couldn't afford to let him affect her like this.

"Meg?"

She ignored the husky sound of his voice and the sensations tripping through her body as she got up from the bed and pulled on her robe. "We'd better get ready. The judging is in an hour."

She stole a glance at Cole. He nodded, but frowned as he got out of bed. Avoiding his gaze, Meg went in to take a shower and forced herself to ignore what had happened there the night before. It was difficult when every tile, every drop of water, and every touch of soap reminded her of their sensuous lovemaking. In fact, she doubted she'd ever be able to take a shower again without remembering. She'd have to switch to baths.

She somehow managed to make it through the shower with her sanity intact, and she finished dressing as Cole showered. It wasn't until they headed out the door, though, that she realized she was just going through the motions and wasn't as interested in Baby's judging as she should be.

Her whole future was riding on this. Why wasn't she more excited—or at least apprehensive? The only thing she felt was relief—relief that it was almost over.

"Ready?" Cole asked.

"Ready."

Cole remained silent and carefully avoided touching her as they headed toward the fairgrounds. Was he worrying about the judging? It was only half an hour away now. Now that the time was closer, Meg began to wonder what the results would be. Would she be doomed to spend the rest of her life rotting away on the farm, or would she be able to follow her dreams?

They entered the barn and made their way toward the rabbit judging area. Not surprisingly, Pops was there. After all, his future was riding on this, too.

Meg felt a pang of remorse, then remembered how Pops had tried to destroy her dreams without giving them a chance. Quickly she glanced around and sighed in relief when she spotted Baby. Good—she'd been afraid Pops had somehow made off with him again. Instead, it appeared he was finally playing it straight.

As she approached him, Pops darted her a look of distress, wringing his hands.

Apprehension filled her. "What's wrong?"

Pops gulped, then blurted out, "Luke's been kidnapped."

Chapter Twelve

Meg stood rooted in shock as she took in her grand-father's words. A cold hand of fear clutched at her heart. No, not Luke. Not that precious, sweet little boy. Who would do such a thing?

"Who?" Cole demanded.

Pops held out a trembling hand with a note in it.

Cole snatched the paper from him and read it. "Beau," he said, expelling the single word like a curse.

"What?" Meg grabbed the note from his hand.

> Natty—I have your son. If you want to see him again, leave the ring in my car on the northwest side of the parking lot at two this afternoon. Don't call the police.

The ring? Yes, it had to be Beau. She glanced at her watch. It was one o'clock now. Just one more hour. "He thinks Natalie has the ring."

"Obviously."

"Does she?"

Cole turned to Pops. "Where's Natalie...and Jerry?"

Pops looked concerned. "They've gone looking for Luke. They left Susie here with me to wait for you, and said if they didn't find him, they'd be back here at a quarter to two."

"Hey, Cole," a voice called.

Meg turned toward the sound, surprised to see Jim and Carol and their kids.

Jim grinned at them. "You made the fair sound like such fun, we thought we'd come up and— What's wrong?"

"Luke's been kidnapped," Cole said. "I need your help, Jim."

Carol reached out to gather her children to her, and Jim's expression turned stony. "You got it. What can I do?"

"Help me search for Luke." Cole turned to Pops. "Does Natalie have the ring?"

"Of course not. I don't know where it is, but she swears she doesn't have it."

When Cole didn't reply, Pops continued. "She wouldn't jeopardize the safety of her son for *that*."

"No. No, she wouldn't," Cole agreed.

He looked harried, frantic, and Meg wanted nothing more than to take away his pain. She felt sick at the thought of what might happen to Luke, and hated to see the anguish Cole was going through.

Grasping for anything that might help, she said, "You don't think Beau would really hurt him, do you?"

Cole shoved a hand through his hair. "I don't know. Two days ago, I would've said he didn't have the guts, but now... I don't know. Men do strange things when they're desperate, and he must be desperate to pull a stunt like this."

Meg shook her head. "Beau's not a monster. He's just stupid. Think about it—Luke would've screamed bloody murder if Beau tried to grab him. Someone would've heard him and reported it. So Luke is probably just fine—and Beau's sitting it out somewhere close by, waiting for Natalie to show up at the car this afternoon."

Cole relaxed a little, and Meg did, too—she just hoped she was right. "So what are we going to do?"

"We?"

"Yes, we. I love Luke, too, and I don't want to have anything happen to him. Maybe I can help."

Cole nodded. "Maybe you can. Carol, can Susie stay here with you?"

Carol nodded.

"Good. Meg—you know what Beau looks like, so you go with Jim. Pops, you come with me. If we don't find them in the next forty-five minutes, we'll meet back here, all right?"

They all nodded, and Cole strode out the door, Jim and Meg right behind him.

"Wait," Pops said, and pointed toward the judging area. "Don't you want to know how Baby did?"

Annoyed, Meg snapped, "Later," and raced out after Jim.

BEAU GLARED at the kid as he wolfed down another corn dog. Nobody'd told him three-year-olds had a bottomless pit when it came to consuming junk food, or that they were such con artists.

He'd thought Luke was gullible, but the anger on the kid's face when he saw there were no puppies had been a lot more daunting than Beau expected. Luckily, he'd had the presence of mind to bribe him with cotton candy before he could let out a peep. And it had been even easier to pay another kid to take a note to Natty.

Since then, they'd continued moving through the fair, Beau watching out for anyone he knew, and Luke keeping an eye out for the most expensive junk food and the most terror-filled rides.

So far, they hadn't run into anyone they knew, but Beau feared it was only a matter of time. He hadn't planned on staging a kidnapping, but Luke didn't know anything about the ring, and it had been the only thing Beau could think of to get his job back.

Luke finished his corn dog and eyed Beau with an avaricious gleam. "Want pop," he announced. "Owange."

Beau sighed and went to buy the kid some orange pop. Just who had kidnapped who, here?

He glanced at his watch. Just a half hour to go. He summoned up a smile. Now to convince the older woman in the booth to watch Luke while Beau retrieved the ring.

COLE MOVED through the fairgrounds at a fast pace, trying not to draw attention to himself, yet scanning every small boy and tall blond man in sight. As he searched, he filled Pops in on the details. The old man kept up easily enough, and Cole began to think he might even be an asset in Beau's capture—if they ever found the creep.

A couple of times, Cole thought he almost had him, but both times the men he accosted were total strangers. With a muttered apology, he moved on.

Forty-five minutes later, Cole conceded defeat. He hadn't found Luke. Though Meg was probably right in believing Beau posed little threat, Cole couldn't help but worry. This was his son. But, for now, their time was up. He urged Pops toward the barn, hoping one of the others had had more luck.

He was the last to arrive. Jim, Meg, Natalie, Jerry, Carol and the kids all looked at him expectantly. Obviously they hadn't found Luke either. His shoulders drooped as he shook his head.

Jim stepped forward. "What now? Shall we call the police?"

Cole shoved a hand through his hair. Should he? "No. Beau said not to—and I don't trust him not to do something crazy if we ignore that. Between the lot of us, we should be able to handle this."

"Okay," Jim agreed. "How?"

"Well, we don't have the ring, so we'll just have to pretend to put one in his car. Natalie, you'll have to do that." He raised an eyebrow at her.

She nodded, wrapping her arms around her waist. "Right. That's what Beau said in the note."

Good. He turned to the others. "I figure the rest of us should lie in wait in the parking lot, encircle him so he can't get away."

He glanced around. "With the six of us, we should be able to stop him." He included Meg and Natalie in the total, knowing they wouldn't stand for being left out. "Carol, can you—?"

"It's all right, Cole. I'll stay here. Do what you have to do."

Cole threw her a swift smile. "Good. Let's go."

He spread them out throughout the parking lot at strategic locations, in case Beau slipped through their fingers and tried to make a run for it. Figuring the kidnapper would be most likely to flee in the opposite direction as soon as possible, Cole positioned himself near the parking lot exit, with Glenda's car handy in case he needed it.

Everyone else was in position and watching Beau's car from their hiding places. Cole glanced at his watch. Two o'clock. He nodded at Natalie, and she walked swiftly to Beau's car, opened the door and placed a small box on the driver's seat. She hung around for a few minutes to see whether Beau would show up, and when he didn't, she left and resumed her watchful position.

Now all they needed was for Beau to show up. Cole shifted from foot to foot, then cursed himself for his impatience. He'd been on many stakeouts before, and had experienced no problem enduring the wait, but this time it was different. This time it was personal, and the stakes were all too high.

Damn. How long had it been? He checked the time. Fifteen minutes. It felt more like an hour. Apparently Beau was being cagey. It made Cole nervous—the more time passed, the more chance there was that something bad would happen to Luke.

Cole glanced up as a man wearing a cowboy hat paused near Beau's car. Cole tensed, then relaxed. That couldn't be Beau . . . or could it?

Oh, yes, it could. No cowboy walked like that.

Before Cole could take a single action, a movement from Jerry's direction spooked Beau, and he bolted, running out of the parking lot, toward the fair—in exactly the opposite direction from Cole.

"That's Beau!" Cole yelled. "Get him!"

The other five came out of their hiding places and surged after the fugitive.

His heart pumping, Cole ran as fast as he could. Jerry was gaining on Beau, but the others were too far behind.

Out of the blue, Cole saw a familiar figure loom right in Beau's path. Hope filled his chest. He knew that man.

"Murphy!" he yelled. "Stop that man!"

Jackson Murphy looked surprised as Beau ran past him, but he took one look at Jerry and tackled him.

Cole cursed inwardly. Damn. Murphy still thought of Jerry as a thief. No wonder he'd taken him out of the action.

Natalie caught up to him and lit into the big man as Jerry lay moaning on the ground. "That's the wrong man!" she screamed, and pointed in the direction of Beau's back. "*He's* the one." Natalie gave Jerry one agonized look, then hurried after Beau.

Murphy appeared chagrined, but Cole couldn't stop to explain. As he ran by, he yelled, "That's okay! Help Jerry, will you? And call the police!"

He didn't stop to see whether Murphy did as he asked. Cole sprinted past Natalie and Pops, never losing sight of Beau's head, bobbing above the crowd as he ran down the midway.

He ducked down an aisle, and Cole followed, passing Meg as he ran. Jim almost caught up to Beau, but a dog darted out, joining the chase. Jim tripped over the mutt and sprawled on the ground.

By the time Cole reached his cousin, he was already on his feet and the dog was gone. Cole glanced around for their quarry. Damn. He'd lost him.

All of a sudden, he saw pink cotton candy flying above the crowd, accompanied by loud cursing. Beau.

Cole and Jim took off in that direction, and the crowd parted, giving them a view of an irate cotton candy vendor, his wares strewn all over the ground...and all over Beau.

Beau glanced back in wide-eyed panic, shedding clouds of pink fluff as he ran. When he saw them, he let out a sound halfway between a moan and a screech and darted into the nearest attraction—the fun house.

As he ran by, the ticket taker yelled, "Hey, you! Come back here! You have to pay!"

Jim and Cole ignored him as they leaped over the turnstiles and hotfooted it after Beau. As he rushed in, Cole had time to notice that two man-size rabbit statues guarded the entrance and exit with open arms. It figured, he thought irreverently. Rabbits again.

"Pops will pay!" he shouted over his shoulder, counting on Meg to make sure everything was set right. "Natalie, guard the exit!"

He and Jim entered the building and stopped. Where had Beau gone? There was a hall of mirrors to the right, and a large spinning disk on the left. He scanned the disk area. Beau wasn't there. He had to be in the mirrors.

Cole gestured Jim to the right, and they ran down the hall. Jim glanced down one corridor and shouted, "There he is!" He charged full tilt after him, only to thud headfirst into a mirror.

Cole winced in sympathy as Jim collapsed, holding his head. Cole took a step toward Jim, but he said, "Don't worry about me. Get Beau."

"Cole? Jim? Where are you?" Meg called.

"In here—in the mirrors," Cole answered, but didn't wait for her. He raced through the hall of mirrors, more careful now that he knew their danger.

He came to the end and paused. There were three paths to choose from. He glanced at all three, and spotted Beau shoving his way past other people to run unevenly across a wildly gyrating catwalk on the other side.

He shot a frantic look at his pursuer, and Cole's mouth firmed into a straight line. He had him now. He dashed to the catwalk and rode the wild surges and swells to the other side, keeping Beau in sight as the kidnapper stumbled through a spinning barrel and out the far end.

Cole sprinted toward the barrel and through it, stopping when he heard a scream. He darted a glance over his shoulder. Natalie lurched on the moving path behind Meg, screeching when a burst of air blew her dress up over her knees. Damn. Why couldn't she wear jeans like Meg?

And what was she doing there, anyway? She was supposed to be guarding the exit. Ignoring his ex-wife's distress, Cole turned to scan the room for Beau. He spotted him approaching the rapidly spinning disk.

The disk filled the whole room except for a crescent-shaped area at the entrance and exit, so the only way to get out was to wait until it stopped spinning, or sit down and ride it until it spun you off at the right angle. If you hit the sides, the walls curved in sharply to thrust you back onto the disk.

Of course, Beau tried a third way—he attempted to run across it. Naturally, he fell and now lay spread-eagled, frantically trying to lever himself to an upright position.

Cole tried to gauge the exact spot to enter, and leaped onto the spinning disk. He miscalculated and fell short, a couple of feet from Beau. Beau kicked at him and missed, then slid outward. He hit the wall and spun back onto the disk, belly up, on the opposite side of Cole.

Cole heard two thumps as the women joined him on the whirling ride. Meg sprawled next to Cole, and Natalie landed right on top of Beau, their arms and legs entangled in what looked like some strange mating ritual.

"That's it—hold on to him!" Cole yelled.

Beau grunted and shoved Natalie away. Natalie clutched at him, but missed and went flying off in the wrong direction. Back she flew toward the entrance, clutching her skirt and screaming all the way.

Damn. Another one down.

He turned to see Meg holding on with determination and moving toward the center. That was it—that was what he had to do. Head for the center, then you could go anywhere from there. As the wheel continued to turn, Cole crept toward the middle.

Just as they reached it, the spinning slowed. Beau flailed for purchase, trying frantically to edge away from them without hitting the wall. He didn't move fast enough, and Cole lunged to grab his foot.

Beau yelped and kicked out, then went sailing off the disk, minus one shoe. As luck would have it, he flew directly toward the exit.

Cole and Meg had to wait one more revolution, but were able to slide off the slowing disk without mishap. As Cole scrambled to his feet, Beau headed out the door.

No...he couldn't get away now. Running after him, Cole charged out the doorway, only to see a leg shoot out from behind one of the guard bunnies. Beau tripped, his head hitting the rabbit's arm with a thunk.

He went down for the count, and Pops stepped out from behind the statue, shaking his head and grinning.

"Whoa, dude," a young voice said behind them. "Did you see that rabbit coldcock that guy?"

Cole smiled grimly and slapped the old man on the back. "Good job." While they all chased Beau through the fun house, Pops had played it smart and remained outside to catch him when he came out. Luckily, not too many people had been looking in this direction.

Cole stared down at Beau as Meg, Natalie and Jim came running up to join them. Now what? Beau wasn't even conscious to tell them what he'd done with Luke.

They were beginning to draw a crowd, so Cole drawled, "So, Pops, did Sonny here have a few too many again?"

A gleam appeared in the old man's eyes, and he played along. "I'm afraid so. Think we ought to take him home to sleep it off?"

"Good idea," Cole agreed. "Jim?"

He and Jim hoisted Beau up, slinging his arms over their shoulders, and walked him toward the exit as the others followed.

"What are we going to do with him?" Jim whispered.

"We'll figure something out. First, let's take him to the parking lot and stick him in the truck until he comes to."

They hauled Beau's unconscious body to the parking lot, picking up Murphy and Jerry along the way. Cole dumped Beau in the back of the truck and waited for him to regain consciousness. With all seven of them standing around watching him, there was no way he'd escape this time.

After about ten minutes, Beau finally began to come to. He opened his eyes and stared in shock, mouth open.

Cole hopped in the back of the truck and straddled Beau's chest. Grabbing his ruffled dress shirt, he demanded, "Where's my son?"

Beau's eyes widened even more, and he didn't even pretend bravery as he gasped out, "Corn dog booth."

Cole's eyes narrowed. "If you're lying—"

"Daddy, Daddy!" came the voice Cole had feared he would never hear again.

He looked up to see Luke waving at him from Carol's arms, as a large woman wearing a mustard-covered apron watched with grudging approval.

"Luke!" Relieved to see his son safe and apparently unharmed, Cole released Beau and ran over to grab his son into his arms.

Meg and Natalie joined them, and Natalie clucked over the boy.

Quickly Cole checked his young son over. There didn't appear to be any injuries. "You okay, sport?"

"My tummy hurts."

Cole snatched up Luke's shirt to check for signs of abuse, but didn't see anything—anything visible, that is.

Carol chuckled. "He didn't mean outside—he meant inside. It seems young Luke here conned Beau into letting him eat everything in sight. I'm afraid he isn't going to feel well for a while."

Cole grinned in relief and turned Luke over to his mother. The others seemed to have the situation well in hand, and were reading Beau the riot act. Murphy, especially, seemed to have Beau terrified.

Now that Luke was safely ensconced in his mother's arms, Cole turned to Carol. "How'd you find him?"

She shrugged. "Pure luck. Beau had left him in a nearby booth, and I just happened to see him when I headed toward the parking lot."

"Thanks, Carol. You see, Meg, why I don't want to raise my son in a big city?"

She needed to follow her dreams, true, but the same was true of him. And his dream was a happy, safe childhood for his son.

"Yes," Meg said simply, and hugged him. "I understand."

The cops arrived then, and Jerry, Jim and Murphy explained the situation while Carol and Natalie escorted the kids out of the parking lot.

Cole elected to stay out of the mess. The others seemed to have the situation well in hand, and he wasn't sure he could keep from strangling Beau if he went near him. Besides, now that Luke was safe, he'd much rather stay near Meg for as long as he could, since he probably wouldn't see her anymore after today.

Meg looked up as her grandfather joined them and hugged the old man. "Thanks, Pops. You were wonderful. I didn't know you had it in you."

He shrugged. "I can move pretty fast when I've a mind to. I'm not as bad off as you think, child."

Cole grinned. He hadn't thought he'd ever hear Pops admit that, but apparently the adrenaline rush of the chase had done the man a world of good. He even looked better—and proud of himself, too.

Meg just raised an eyebrow, and Pops gazed down at the ground, a long look on his face. "I have something else to tell you."

"What? What's wrong?"

"Baby won."

It almost hurt to see the way Meg's face lit up at the news. "Did he win the third leg?" she asked.

Pops nodded. "Yep, the leg, and the grand championship." He grasped Meg's shoulder. "I'm proud of you, Meggie. You said them rabbits was worth something, and you was right. I'm sorry I doubted you."

Meg hugged him around the neck. "It's okay, Pops."

She released him, and he shuffled his feet and glanced down at them, mumbling, "And I'm right sorry about the bet. You won fair and square. It'll take me a little time to sell the farm—"

"It's okay, Pops," she said softly. "You don't have to."

The old man's face lit with hope. "You mean—?"

She nodded and gave him a sad smile. "Yes. I'm releasing you from the bet."

The old man whooped and waved his hat in the air. "You're a good girl, Meggie." He ran to tell Jerry the good news.

That meant Cole was alone—sort of—in the parking lot with Meg. He squeezed her shoulder and tilted her chin up so that her gaze met his. "That was a nice thing to do."

She shrugged. "Not really."

"Yes, it was. You just gave up your dream for your family. Why?"

She kept her gaze averted, watching as Jerry apparently shared Pops's enthusiasm for the news. "Well, after going through the terror of Luke's kidnapping,

I realized how important family is." She glanced over sadly as the two men rejoiced. "And raising rabbits is *their* dream. How can I deprive them of that?"

"What about yours? You could still move to San Antonio on your own—"

She shook her head.

"No, hear me out. I'll be in Lingston, so I can make sure your brother and grandfather are taken care of. If nothing else, I'll hire someone to do that."

She looked at him in awe. "You'd do that for me?"

He kissed her uptilted nose. "Don't you know by now that I'd do anything for you?"

Tears formed in Meg's eyes, and she wiped them away, then hugged Cole around the neck. "That's the nicest thing anyone's ever said to me."

Cole's heart wrenched as he held her close. He loved her, so he had to do what was best for her, no matter how much it hurt. "So, you're going to take me up on it?"

Meg smiled at him through her tears. "No."

"No?"

"No. I changed my mind about moving to San Antonio."

"You changed your mind? Just like that?" Hope and disbelief stabbed through him.

"No, not just like that." She smiled again. "I've had more than my share of excitement these past few days—and the experience is highly overrated. In fact, it's downright frightening at times."

His eyebrows rose. "I agree, but I never thought I'd hear you say that."

"Well, I did," she said. "Say, did you mean it when you said you'd do anything for me?"

"Of course." How could she doubt him?

"Well, Mr. McKenzie, you'd better hold your weekends free for the next several months. I figure dating you is going to be excitement enough."

Cole grinned, then let out a whoop of his own as he picked Meg up and swung her around. He halted and stared down into her face. "You won't regret it, I promise. I love you, Meg."

Meg smiled up at him. "Oh, Cole, I love you, too," she said and gave him a kiss that proved it.

Their happiness was interrupted by a shout. Cole turned to look as Jerry bent down to pick something up from the truck bed. "Hey, everyone," he called. "Guess what I found caught on a bit of ribbon under the feed box?"

As everyone watched, Jerry held up something shiny. "Why, it looks like a diamond ring."

He grinned and turned to look at Beau. As Beau watched with a horrified look on his face, Jerry placed the ring on Natalie's hand and looked soulfully into her eyes.

Beau lunged toward the couple, his eyes mad with frenzy. "No, that's my ring! Mine! Mine!"

The cops restrained him, then cuffed him as Beau kept his eyes fixed on the ring, screaming, "Noooooo!"

Meg turned to Cole. "You're not really going to let him go to jail, are you?"

"No," Cole said with a smile. "I think Beau's been punished enough. Besides, I have plans for that ring. Special plans."

Epilogue

Meg dried the last dish and put it in the drainer, then smiled as Cole came up behind her to kiss her on the neck. She returned the embrace and sighed in happiness. "Do you realize that only one short year ago today, I believed my life was over because I couldn't move to San Antonio?"

Cole just nuzzled her neck some more. "Yes, but it took me three more months to convince you to marry me—even after I bought you that whopper of an engagement ring."

Meg glanced fondly at the diamond that had brought them together. "Yes, but everything turned out wonderfully. We have Luke and Lady—"

"And Natalie has settled right in with Pops and Jerry."

Meg shifted slightly so that his badge wouldn't chafe her. "Their marriage is turning out wonderfully. All Natalie wanted was someone to need and adore her. She needed someone helpless and dependent...like my family."

Meg chuckled and kissed him, loving the way it still thrilled her, even after nine months of marriage. "Sounds like a great trade to me."

Cole hugged her tighter. "So, what are we doing this weekend?"

She smiled. Living in Lingston with Cole certainly wasn't boring. She didn't know why she hadn't seen it before, but he was already that perfect blend of Steven Seagal and Tom Hanks, of Rambo and the boy next door.

And she was still "dependable old Meg," but now, at least twice a month, Cole had an outing planned or let her choose one. Luckily, it didn't take much to satisfy her craving for adventure anymore. A visit to Sea World, a short trek to the coast or to Austin to visit his wonderful family, or even just a picnic on the back porch, more than sufficed.

She moved to the refrigerator and pulled out a bottle of sparkling grape juice. "We're not going anywhere this weekend, but we are going to celebrate."

"Celebrate? Celebrate what? Wait, I know. The one-year anniversary of the day we met?"

"No," Meg said, and turned to her wonderful, sexy husband with eyes full of love. "We're celebrating the fact that Luke is going to have a younger brother or sister."

Cole's eyes widened, and his mouth dropped open. "We're going to have a baby?" he asked in awe and delight.

She nodded, and Cole grabbed her to whirl her around the kitchen in dizzying circles of happiness.

Meg laughed in pure joy, content in knowing that Gram would approve. Meg *had* fulfilled her dream. It had just taken her a while to realize that excitement and happiness came in small things—like having picnics, making love, and chasing babies.

When all the evidence points to love,
there's only one verdict.

VERDICT:
Matrimony

Witness the power of love this September as
seasoned courtroom lawyers discover that
sometimes there's just no defense against love.

This special collection of three complete stories
by your favorite authors makes a compelling
case for love.

WITHOUT PRECEDENT by JoAnn Ross
VOICES IN THE WIND by Sandra Canfield
A LEGAL AFFAIR by Bobby Hutchinson

Available this September wherever Harlequin
and Silhouette books are sold.

HARLEQUIN ® ♥ *Silhouette*®

HREQ0996

National Bestselling Author

JoANN ROSS

Welcomes you to Raintree, Georgia—
steamy capital of sin, scandal and murder.

Southern Comforts

Chelsea Cassidy is the official biographer of
Roxanne Scarbrough—the Southern Queen of good
taste who's built an empire around the how-to's of
gracious living. It's clear to Chelsea that somebody
wants her employer dead.

As Chelsea explores the dark secrets of Roxanne's
life, the search leads Chelsea into the arms of
Cash Beaudine. And now her investigating becomes
personal with potentially fatal consequences.

Available this September wherever books are sold.

A woman with a shocking secret.
A man without a past.
Together, their love could be nothing less than

Scandalous

The latest romantic adventure from

CANDACE CAMP

When a stranger suffering a loss of memory lands on Priscilla Hamilton's doorstep, her carefully guarded secret is threatened. Always a model of propriety, she knows that no one would believe the deep, dark desire that burns inside her at this stranger's touch.

As scandal and intrigue slowly close in on the lovers, will their attraction be strong enough to survive?

Find out this September at your favorite retail outlet.

MIRA **The brightest star in women's fiction**   MCCSC

Look us up on-line at:http://www.romance.net

REBECCA YORK

43 LIGHT STREET

FACE TO FACE

Bestselling author Rebecca York returns to "43 Light Street" for an original story of past secrets, deadly deceptions—and the most intimate betrayal.

She woke in a hospital—with amnesia...and with child. According to her rescuer, whose striking face is the last image she remembers, she's Justine Hollingsworth. But nothing about her life seems to fit, except for the baby inside her and Mike Lancer's arms around her. Consumed by forbidden passion and racked by nameless fear, she must discover if she is Justine...or the victim of some mind game. Her life—and her unborn child's—depends on it....

Don't miss *Face To Face*—Available in October, wherever Harlequin books are sold.

HARLEQUIN®

®

43FTF

Look us up on-line at: http://www.romance.net

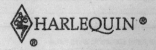

HARLEQUIN®

...equin favorites by some of our most

...can receive a discount by ordering two or more titles!

HT #25663	THE LAWMAN by Vicki Lewis Thompson	* $3.25 U.S. ☐/$3.75 CAN. ☐
HP #11788	THE SISTER SWAP by Susan Napier	$3.25 U.S. ☐/$3.75 CAN. ☐
HR #03293	THE MAN WHO CAME FOR CHRISTMAS by Bethany Campbell	$2.99 U.S. ☐/$3.50 CAN. ☐
HS #70667	FATHERS & OTHER STRANGERS by Evelyn Crowe	$3.75 U.S. ☐/$4.25 CAN. ☐
HI #22198	MURDER BY THE BOOK by Margaret St. George	$2.89 ☐
HAR #16520	THE ADVENTURESS by M.J. Rodgers	$3.50 U.S. ☐/$3.99 CAN. ☐
HH #28885	DESERT ROGUE by Erin Yorke	$4.50 U.S. ☐/$4.99 CAN. ☐

(limited quantities available on certain titles)

	AMOUNT	$
DEDUCT:	10% DISCOUNT FOR 2+ BOOKS	$
ADD:	POSTAGE & HANDLING	$
	($1.00 for one book, 50¢ for each additional)	
	APPLICABLE TAXES**	$_____
	TOTAL PAYABLE	$_____
	(check or money order—please do not send cash)	

To order, complete this form and send it, along with a check or money order for the total above, payable to Harlequin Books, to: **In the U.S.:** 3010 Walden Avenue, P.O. Box 9047, Buffalo, NY 14269-9047; **In Canada:** P.O. Box 613, Fort Erie, Ontario, L2A 5X3.

Name: _____

Address: _____ City: _____

State/Prov.: _____ Zip/Postal Code: _____

**New York residents remit applicable sales taxes.
  Canadian residents remit applicable GST and provincial taxes.   HBACK-JS3

Look us up on-line at: http://www.romance.net